Living Dreams

Partha Mazumdar

Leadstart
INKSTATE

ISBN 978-93-56103-89-4
Copyright © Partha Mazumdar

First published in India 2022 by Leadstart Inkstate
A brand of One Point Six Technologies Pvt. Ltd.

123, Building J2, Shram Seva Premises,
Wadala Truck Terminal,
Mumbai 400022, Maharashtra, INDIA
Phone: +91 96999 33000
Email: info@leadstartcorp.com
www.leadstartcorp.com

Disclaimer: This is a work of fiction. All the names, characters, businesses, places, events and incidents in this book are either the product of the author's imagination or used in a fictitious manner. Any resemblance to actual persons, living or dead, or actual events is purely coincidental.

Editor: Roona Ballachanda
Cover: Ilaya Raja
Layouts: Sathish Kumar

To Ma

Contents

About the Author

Partha is an Indian-Australian author living in Melbourne. A Bengali babu at heart, he was born in Kolkata. He spent the first thirty years of his life in Kolkata / Delhi and then migrated to Australia in 1998. He completed his MBA from Monash University in 2000. His working life started in the early 90s as a MIS Trainee in a large company and then moved to Finance and Merchant Banking.

In Australia, he has been a part of a few start-up companies and also worked for one of the big banks in various capacities. About 10 yrs ago, he decided to go on his own, helping small and medium businesses with their web and online requirements. About three years ago, he floated his own start up in real-estate space, which had been his dream for a long time.

The industry downturn due to covid made him rethink his future direction. Many of his clients closed their shop and income for him became scarce. His dream came crashing down and he decided to close shop to minimise his losses. He started writing small blogs and articles, mainly in the space of Business and Economics to keep himself busy, as he searched for work.

About a year ago, he was encouraged by a friend to participate in a digital release of a mosaic of short stories. His story was well accepted by his readers. That was when he decided to take up some serious writing. This book is a fictional presentation of his beliefs and values that he has grown up with. Circumstances brought out the writer in him. He loves writing and is dreaming about a second and a third book.

Acknowledgements

I would like to express my gratitude and thank three lovely ladies in my life who helped me enormously in my writing journey.

I am highly indebted to my sister Kaberi who has constantly held my hand, guided me and helped me streamline my thought process. She is a great listener and I have bounced all my ideas off her. She has inspired me to write this book.

My lovely daughter Annika, who has always been by my side, gave me ideas and has been a big morale booster. I know she will be very proud of me when she sees this book published.

And of course, this book wouldn't have been possible without the support of my wife, Dipika.

The Spice Connect

<h1 style="text-align:center">Chapter 1</h1>

Return Journey

It was the beginning of summer, start of the travel season in Australia. Tullamarine Airport was crowded. Robin and Nandini managed to clear immigration and security well on time. They still had more than an hour in hand before boarding. They walked towards the boarding gate when Nandini stopped in front of a departure display board and looked up. She seemed completely lost. Robin checked. Their flight to Kolkata was on time.

Robin was watching Nandini closely. He could imagine well what his wife was going through. He held her hand gently and asked, "Do you want to buy something from the duty free…for *baba* (father)?"

"No," she replied. Nandini quickly took control of herself. Pointing to a quiet corner she said, "Let's go and sit there. I am feeling a bit tired." Robin agreed with a nod. Nandini walked to the end of a long row of seats and Robin followed her.

This was the first time they were flying out of Melbourne after their wedding and that too, to Kolkata, Nandini's city. For the newly wedded couple, this was not what they had dreamt of. It was exactly the opposite.

Nandini sat next to the big glass window and Robin sat beside her. Nandini looked comfortable but she was still very quiet. She was observing all the activities outside, on the tarmac. Loaders were loading up all the luggage, the oil tanker operator connected the fuel pipe to the aircraft and was filling up for the next journey and the ground engineer was completing the aircraft inspection. Robin, on the other hand, was interested in the bright lights of the duty free shops around them.

Robin held Nandini's hand once again. He wanted Nandini to be normal and be the talkative girl she had always been. This time he succeeded!

"Looks like everybody has a role to play." Nandini said with a faint smile.

"What do you mean?" Robin wanted to take the conversation further.

"Well, look outside, all those guys working on the ground, they are doing different jobs, but they have one single goal – help people reach their destination! It hardly matters to them who is going where and why. Do you think any of these guys have ever been to Kolkata?"

"I don't think so." Robin promptly answered.

After a brief pause, Nandini continued, "See how focused they are on their job. Did you see that guy there, he slipped on the tarmac and the other guys came running? They helped him get up on his feet and they are back, doing their job."

She took her eyes off those guys, looked up at a distance and continued, "I guess they will continue to work till their job is done, rain or sun, winter or summer."

Robin agreed and shifted his focus from the duty-free shops to activities outside.

After a brief pause, he said, "Yes, true, that is their job. So, what is your point?"

Nandini gently placed her head on his shoulder, "Nothing great… I think…just like them, we also have a role to play as individuals. We may stumble and fall but we shouldn't lose sight of our goal. We have all come to this world for a reason and will leave this earth once our duty is over." She said that pointing at an aircraft that had just taken off from the runway.

Robin held Nandini's hand firmly, "Listen love, I can understand why you are thinking like this, but we have 12 hours of flying ahead of us. You have lots of duties to perform once you reach Kolkata. Just remember – Time is the best healer."

Nandini agreed and tried to be normal. Robin said, "You look gorgeous in a *saree*. The last time you wore one was on our wedding day!"

Nandini turned her head towards him and smiled. She could barely hold back her tears. "Yes, and *Ma* (mother) helped me wear it. She was the one, who asked me to wear a *saree*, when I visit Kolkata next. And by the way she also said that you should be wearing *dhuti punjabi*. (A dress worn by Bengali men on special occasions.)"

"Why didn't you tell me that? I would have worn one!"

"Are you serious? Remember how uncomfortable you were on our wedding day? You were concentrating more on keeping the dhuti tied to your waist than the wedding rituals. It would have become a real scene at the airport today!" Nandini laughed as she visualised the scene.

"So what? I would have managed somehow knowing the kind of attention I would get!" Robin laughed heartily.

"You attention seeker…" Nandini checked Robin and said, "I am sure you would have managed if you knew it was ma's wish but now *ma* is not there to receive her *jamai* (son-in-law)…so it's okay" Nandini's voice choked but she controlled herself.

"You don't know Robin, what plans *ma* had for us! She wanted to give you a grand welcome when you visited your *shoshur bari* (in-laws' house) for the first time."

Robin smiled, "I know but I' m sure my dad-in-law must have planned something for my welcome! Are you sure you don't want to do any last-minute duty-free shopping?"

Nandini shook her head, "nope."

Robin felt sad for Nandini. She had planned a lot for their first trip to Kolkata after marriage. She had a long shopping list. She wanted to carry gifts for all her relatives and friends but before she could even start shopping it was time for them to leave for Kolkata!

Next came the boarding announcement. Nandini stood up instantly as the announcement was being made, but then realised it wasn't for her. It was for passengers with children and those who required special assistance!

"Not us." Nandini felt embarrassed.

"You seem to be in a hurry," said Robin

Nandini smiled and sat down and waited for the next announcement. She was in a hurry! She was in a hurry to meet her *baba* (father). He must be having a tough time without her mother. He had always been lost in his books and never bothered about worldly matters. It was Nandini's mother who managed everything – the house, the relatives and even the finance!

"*Baba* must be feeling so lost without *ma*," Nandini muttered to herself.

"Did you say something?" Robin asked

"Nothing, just thinking aloud," Nandini smiled.

Finally, they boarded the flight. Nandini got the window seat.

The journey began. The aircraft taxied across the long runway. There was a queue of aircrafts to take off. After a long wait, theirs was finally ready for take-off. As the flight took off, the city underneath faded gradually. It gained height, and in a few minutes, was flying over the clouds. They couldn't see the city anymore, just white cottony clouds.

"*Ma* must be somewhere here among the clouds…" Nandini thought.

After a long eight-hour flight, they landed in Singapore, early morning the next day.

A couple of hours later, they boarded their flight to Kolkata.

As they got closer to Kolkata, Robin noticed Nandini was becoming more active. She was smiling more and trying to look happy, but her eyes were still teary. She was trying very hard to hold them back.

Their flight finally landed at Netaji Subhas Chandra Bose International Airport, Kolkata.

Nandini took a deep breath "Yes I can smell it!" she said.

"What?" asked Robin.

"The smell of Kolkata, the smell of my soil, the smell of Bangla…you won't understand Mr. Australian. Leave it…" said Nandini with a grin on her face.

Robin took a deep breath like Nandini and said, "No dear… I can also smell something in the air."

"You can? See I told you, air in Kolkata is different. What does it smell like?"

"I don't know what it is, but I think the air smells like fish fried in mustard oil and trust me it's yummy." Nandini knew Robin was just teasing her.

They walked out of the aircraft. The air was warm and humid and not at all comfortable for Robin, but he felt good because Nandini was happy.

"I am coming back to Kolkata after two years." Said Nandini to the immigration officer, the security officer and every other person she interacted with. She had a spring in her steps.

Robin greeted all airport officials in Bengali. He was out to prove his Bengali heritage. Everybody loved the fact that Robin, a white foreigner was speaking Bengali fluently! This Bengali *bhadralok* (gentleman) looked very different.

They picked up their luggage, cleared immigration and were walking out of the Airport.

As they came out of the airport, the local taxi drivers swarmed them like bees.

Nandini looked for her *baba* in the crowd and there he was…standing quietly behind the crowd.

"*Nandu, ami ekhane* (Nandu, I am here)." He said, waving his hand high up in the air.

Nandini ran to her *baba* like a little girl and hugged him tight. All the tears that she had held back during the whole journey and maybe longer, came out. She cried her heart out.

Tears rolled down her father's cheeks too. But he kept a gentle smile on his face.

He was very happy that Nandini and Robin were in Kolkata but deep in his heart, he was crying. He was missing Nandini's mother. He could never have imagined in his wildest of nightmares that Nandini's mother would not be there to receive her daughter!

"How much your mother planned for her daughter and son-in-law's first visit to Kolkata! I couldn't do anything..." Nandini's father said.

"What can you do *baba*? Things don't always happen according to our wish." Nandini tried to pacify her father.

Nandini and her father suddenly realized that a crowd of people had gathered around them to witness the father-daughter reunion and Robin stood unattended not knowing what to do.

Nandini's father quickly turned to Robin and said, "Hope you had a comfortable flight, Robin!"

"Yes, thank you," he replied.

Robin, not sure how to react came closer and folded his hands to greet his father-in-law. Nandini acted fast and touched her father's feet. Robin followed suit. Nandini's father blessed them both. It was time to go home.

They started walking towards the car park. Nandini suddenly stopped, came close to Robin, held his hand and turned around facing the airport terminal. She whispered, *"This is where my journey began two years ago."* Pointing her finger to the airport terminal.

Kolkata – The City of Joy

Chapter 2

The Journey

(Two years earlier)

Nandini was a Kolkata girl and the only child of her parents. She completed her Master's degree in computer science from a reputed institute in Kolkata. She received a few on-campus job offers from big companies in Bangalore and Gurgaon but she refused them because she wanted to be in Kolkata! After struggling for a couple of months, she landed a job at a small web development company in Kolkata. She was happy that she could live with her parents and meet her friends regularly.

She worked for six months there and realised that the company wasn't the right one for her. Being a topper in the University, she wanted something more challenging, with better growth prospects.

She belonged to a typical middle class progressive Bengali family. Her dad worked as a botany professor at the Kolkata University and her mother was a home maker. He had a couple of more years of service left before retirement.

Tired and frustrated with the work situation, Nandini finally decided to apply for jobs with companies outside

Kolkata. She landed a job with one of the multinational IT companies in Bangalore and her first project was with a major Bank in Melbourne.

Her parents were a bit hesitant. She was their only child and had never visited outside Kolkata by herself, let alone live in a foreign country for a long period of time.

Her dad asked, "How long is the project for?"

"Six months" replied she.

Her dad asked again, "Do you really want to do this job?"

Nandini nodded. Her father could never go against her wishes, so he decided to postpone his decision. He said, "Let me ask your mother. We will discuss it tomorrow."

That night Nandini got very disturbed. She heard her parents discussing about getting her married before she left. That way, they would be at peace, knowing that their daughter was married and not alone in faraway Australia.

But Nandini wasn't ready yet for marriage. She wanted to see the world, explore more opportunities and be financially independent before getting married. Moreover, she didn't quite like the idea of arranged marriage. How could a girl and a boy decide to get married by just meeting once! She wanted to fall in love before marriage.

Before the discussion could start the next day and before her parents could take any action, Nandini told them that she wasn't going alone. There was another girl from Delhi who was going for the same project and was also unmarried. The company would provide them accommodation and take care of all their needs, so there was nothing to worry. It was a matter of only six months!

Nandini's parents had little choice but to agree. They had a couple of conditions. Nandini had to promise that she wouldn't get into any relationship with a foreigner, and she would return to Kolkata after six months.

She agreed to both the conditions. Melbourne was going to be Nandini's first destination outside India. She was excited but nervous. She spent a couple of days before her departure, shopping for warm clothes, some formals and a few cooking utensils.

Her parents came to see her off at the Airport. As Nandini touched her parent's feet to get their blessings, they became very emotional. Her father was very quiet. Her mother cried hugging her tightly. Nandini also felt sad, but she managed to hold back her tears and said, "*Ma eto kedo na* (Ma don't cry so much). Your daughter is not going to her *shoshur-bari* (in-law's house) she is going to build her career. Hold your tears for that day *ma* (mother)."

Nandini's mother laughed at her daughter's advice. She wiped her tears and said with a smile, "You won't understand my feelings till you become a mother Nandu. Be careful always and take care of yourself. I will call you every day. Please remember to pick up my phone and…"

Nandini hugged her mother tight to stop her. "Don't worry *ma* it's only for six months!"

Nandini walked into the Airport. She was travelling alone for the first time in her life!

Her project partner, Padma would take her flight from Delhi and join her in Singapore. From there they would fly together.

As planned, Nandini met Padma in Singapore. They became friends in no time. It was Padma's first overseas trip too.

They arrived in Melbourne late at night. An office representative welcomed them at the airport and dropped them at their accommodation, one of the serviced apartments in the heart of the city. Their initial stay there was for 3 weeks. Thereafter, they would have to find their own rental accommodations.

Nandini and Padma settled well at their workplace. Nandini enjoyed working on the new project. People were good and friendly. The work culture was very different from that in Kolkata. Melbourne city was also very different from Kolkata. The city and the air were cleaner, cars were bigger and faster, buildings were taller, and the city got deserted after 6 in the evening.

Nandini felt like a stranger in the city. Only one thing made her feel at home – the Melbourne trams! They reminded her of trams in Kolkata. The Kolkata trams looked older than the trams here though!

Nandini's office was just a 10-minute walk from her apartment. Usually, Padma and she would walk to their office together. After finishing work, they would go to one of the restaurants in China town, get something to eat and then walk back home. On their way Nandini would always stop and stare at the moving trams. One day, Padma suggested that they should hop into one and take a ride. Nandini's feeling of homesickness might reduce to some extent that way. So Nandini and Padma hopped in to one of them while on their way back from work one evening.

As they hopped in, they realized there were only a few people inside, mostly tourists. Nandini took out her purse, hoping to buy tickets but soon they found that tram travel was free within the Melbourne city boundaries!

Nandini chose to sit at the rear of the tram. Padma followed her. Nandini had always enjoyed travelling in a tram and now even more because it was free!

Sitting in the tram, Nandini went back to her childhood days when she would take tram rides with her father on weekends and holidays, especially during *Durga Puja* celebrations. He would often tell little Nandini that the tram was like a big python, crawling gently on the tracks, carrying passengers in its belly. It was a friendly python that was slow but didn't pollute the air, so those who loved the earth loved trams!

The tram rides became a time for father-daughter bonding! As Nandini grew up the frequency of their tram rides became less, and discussions became more serious. Now they would discuss more about economics, history, politics, and current affairs. The discussions often turned into debates. Nandini would put across her thoughts so powerfully that her father would be surprised! He couldn't believe his little princess had grown up so quickly and held such strong views!

Nandini remembered everything. She narrated her father's python story to Padma. She observed though that the Melbourne trams were a bit bigger and wider than their Kolkata counterparts. Also, they were air-conditioned and less noisy.

'You know what, I think the Melbourne trams are more an anaconda than a python.' she smiled and told Padma.

Nandini and Padma enjoyed watching the city from inside the tram. Suddenly Nandini spotted a rather strange, very old looking tram, approaching them on the opposite track. It looked old, wooden, and red in colour.

"Now, that looks like a very old version," Nandini told Padma, pointing at the red tram.

"Hmm, we should travel in one of those, next time," Padma replied with a nod.

Nandini did a bit of research on the red trams on Melbourne streets. 'The trams were about 100 years old. They were restored and kept in service after years of lobbying by heritage and public transport supporters. An average of three million passengers travelled in the red trams every year, with each tram circling the city 9 to 12 times a day!'

Next day, they sat in one of the city circle trams. Nandini could instantly relate to the "Australian" version of Kolkata trams. The ride was like the Kolkata trams.

Both girls agreed that the city circle trams were more exciting than the modern trams. Very often they would buy a pack of sandwich each and sit in one of the city circle trams, have a chit chat and take a ride. It was the best way to go around the city.

One day while coming back from work, rather than their usual dinner in the city, they decided to check out the restaurants at Docklands. It is the newer part of Melbourne city, built on swamp land. It is a hub for waterfront dining, retail and entertainment. The restaurants were exquisite, looked quite expensive and represented fine dining. They were lucky that day, one of the restaurants had weekday specials on offer, that evening. All the food was at half price. It was like a jackpot for the girls. Fine dining at half price.

The restaurants usually would get a big crowd on Fridays and weekends. It was a weekday, so there weren't many people around.

They walked in and sat on the pier side, next to a large window with a good view. The restaurant offered Italian and continental dishes. Nandini ordered a chicken risotto while Padma got a vegetarian pasta. It was getting dark slowly as the sun set on the western horizon. The sky turned orange and the girls loved the view.

The restaurant had a very modern set up. The kitchen was behind a big wall of glass. They could see the food being cooked by the chefs. That night in the kitchen, it seemed like there were two chefs and a few helpers. They could easily differentiate the chefs from others. They wore that weird kind of chef's hat.

Nandini was observing the chef, preparing the risotto for her. She was quite impressed with the multi-tasking skills of the chef. He was not only cooking the risotto but also making a couple of pizzas, possibly for one of the other customers. While she followed all his movements in the kitchen, she missed out on the fact that the chef also seemed interested in her. In between his cooking, he would look at Nandini. The more he looked, the harder it got for him to take his eyes off her. It got a bit embarrassing when their eyes locked. She realised that and shifted her gaze, as if nothing had happened.

Padma's pasta was ready for service. The Chef placed the pasta on the service table and rang a bell. One of the waiters served it to her. The girls decided to share the food between them. They got busy and were enjoying the meal while the risotto was still being cooked. Suddenly, Nandini realised that somebody was standing right next to her. She turned; it was the chef himself. He was standing there with a plate.

"Your risotto is ready," he said and put the plate on the table. "Hope you enjoy the meal."

"Thank you" said Nandini. He left them alone, went back to the kitchen and got busy.

The chef was a tall, brown haired and blue-eyed white Australian. Nandini winked at Padma and whispered "Very impressive. Mr. Chef wanted to make us feel very special."

"Not us," Padma winked, "just you." They both laughed.

That night the girls had a good time. The food was good. The chef did come up in their discussion a couple of times, but they just moved on.

As time passed, Nandini and Padma got busy with work. They also moved to the outer suburbs to an accommodation that was cheaper and more spacious. Two other girls also shared the house with them. They now had to travel for hours by train to get to work. Soon they were travelling at different times to different places independently.

Although work kept her busy, Nandini would never miss a chance to take the "city circle tram" ride, before heading home. She didn't want to lose that connection with Kolkata.

One fine evening after work, Nandini bought a chicken sandwich, and got in her favourite tram for a ride to the Melbourne Central Station. She was enjoying her sandwich and the outside view, as the tram rolled on the tracks through Docklands. The tram stopped and two young men hopped in. One of them looked like an Indian and the other was a white Australian "Blue eyed" boy!

Nandini could immediately connect, "Isn't that the chef at the restaurant who made my risotto!" she asked herself. He surely was. By then he had recognised Nandini and was smiling at her. Nandini felt a bit uncomfortable. She didn't know how to react. She looked out of the window, ignoring him.

Nandini felt as if "Mr. Chef" was staring at her, at times. On a couple of occasions, their eyes did meet, "nope I shouldn't do this" she thought. His friend of course, was more interested in his mobile phone.

As the tram approached Melbourne Central Station, Nandini stood up to get out of the tram. The two men stood up too. They walked behind her and talked in whispers. Nandini was sure that they were following her. She started walking faster. As she walked onto the platform, the two men were right in front of her, as if waiting for her.

The chef walked up to her and said "Hi, my name is Robin, the chef at the restaurant, remember?"

She wanted to avoid him, but the platform was very crowded, not an inch of space to move. She hesitatingly said "yes". Then she looked here and there, trying to move away, but couldn't.

Robin asked politely, "Are you a Bengali?"

She was kind of puzzled. What does he know about Bengalis and why the hell was he bothered about her being a Bengali? She asked back, "How does it matter?"

Robin smiled back as if he was sure of what he was asking. By then, the train had arrived. Nandini quickly boarded the train and found herself a seat. She didn't look back to see if Robin or his friend had boarded the train or not. She wanted to send him a message that she wasn't interested at all.

'Whatever it was, Robin had a genuine smile; he couldn't be a ruffian,' Nandini thought. Nevertheless, his question kept on troubling her. Yes, she did look like a Bengali girl because she had big, beautiful eyes but she never thought they were so prominent that even a foreigner could tell that she was a Bengali!!

She remained confused about the incident. She discussed it with her friends. They advised her not to worry. One of them suggested that she should contact the police, if any of the boys ever tried to contact her. As time passed, Nandini forgot about the incident and life became normal again. She shrugged it off as a one-off encounter with a couple of flirtatious characters.

Durga Puja in Melbourne

It was going to be Nandini's first *Durga Puja* (Hindu festival paying homage to Goddess Durga), away from Kolkata. She was missing Kolkata a lot. In one of the calls, her mother said, "You have worked enough Nandu, now come back. *Ma* Durga is coming home, you also come back home."

Nandini laughed at her mother and said, "*Ma* you know I can't leave the project halfway. Moreover, your *Ma* Durga comes to Melbourne also. Let me meet her here this year!" Her mother didn't quite like the idea but said nothing further.

Nandini connected with a few Bengalis in Melbourne through Facebook and found out that *Durga Puja* was generally celebrated during the weekends and there were quite a few *Durga Puja* celebrations in and around Melbourne. Nandini chose the one that was the oldest and closest to her.

She asked Padma to accompany her to the *Puja Mandap* (hall) on the first day of celebration. Dressed in a cotton *saree*, Nandini reached the *Puja Mandap*. She was impressed to see so many Bengali people together celebrating their biggest festival, so far away from their homeland! She also made friends with a few people and loved talking in her mother tongue after a long time!

Padma was watching Nandini and everything around. She was attending a Bengali *Durga Puja* celebration for the first time. She loved the idol of Goddess Durga with her four children the most. Nandini explained to her in detail the story of *Ma* Durga's home coming.

It was time for *Pushpanjali* (floral offering to Goddess Durga) and everyone stood in rows facing the idol. Someone had to distribute flowers. Nandini offered to help. She distributed flowers to everyone in a row.

Nandini was in for a big surprise. Standing at the end of the row, were two familiar faces. "Mr. Chef and his Indian friend". The first question that came to her mind, "What are they doing here? Have they been following me?" She quickly gave them flowers and came and stood next to Padma.

"I think Mr. Chef is in love," Padma whispered to Nandini with a smile. The process of *Pushpanjali* (floral offering to Goddess Durga) started and ended with prayers. Nandini had her eyes closed as she prayed "*Ma* Durga, bless me with your strength and wisdom…be with me always"

As she opened her eyes, she saw Robin and his friend standing right in front of her.

Padma was nowhere to be seen.

They greeted her, "Happy *Durga Puja*."

Nandini didn't wish back, she was shocked. Her brain was working overtime, "Hmm one is an Australian and the other a North Indian why would they be at *Durga Puja* Hall?" she was trying to reason out.

"Are you still thinking that we have followed you here?" Robin asked with a bright smile on his face.

"No, not really," Nandini said feeling embarrassed.

Robin continued, "So I was right. You are a Bengali." Nandini just smiled. Without taking the conversation any further, she moved away from them. Robin knew that she was avoiding him.

It was time for having *Bhog* (food offering to Goddess Durga that is distributed to devotees) and Nandini observed that Robin, like everyone else sat and enjoyed it with as much *bhakti* (sincerity) as any other Bengali. He was thinking hard. He wasn't going to give up so easily.

As the day was about to end, Robin gathered all his courage and walked up to Nandini. He asked, "Will you be coming tomorrow?"

Nandini replied instantly, "No we won't."

Robin smiled as if he knew Nandini's answer. "OK but we are coming. Tomorrow is Ashtami and I don't want to miss out on the special dishes on the *Bhog!* (Food offering to the Goddess)" Robin said with a twinkle in his eye.

Now things were quite clear to Nandini. Mr. Chef and his friend were here for the food!

Robin could comprehend Nandini's smile but continued with the same enthusiasm,

"Why don't you visit our restaurant this weekend? We have some good offers on food and drinks. If you don't like Italian, we can go somewhere else, for dinner?" Nandini was intelligent, she knew exactly where the conversation was heading.

Nandini answered in a firm tone, "I don't go out with strangers. I come from a very traditional Bengali family, my parents will never like me getting involved with a foreigner…" she said in one go and without waiting for a reply, she walked away.

Padma heard all of it and thought Nandini was overreacting but before she could comment, Nandini pulled her out of the *Puja* Hall. They left for the day.

The next day Nandini and Padma reached the *Puja* Hall well on time. Nandini came better prepared to encounter Mr. Chef and his friend that day. She planned to show a lot of attitude and if required be rude with them and say, "No".

As expected, the two men were at the *Puja Mandap* too. While having *Pushpanjali* and *Bhog,* Robin tried to talk to Nandini, but she didn't care to even look at him.

Just before going home Robin gathered enough courage to talk to Nandini. "Can I have a word with you?"

"No and whatever you ask my answer will be a big 'No'!" Nandini answered as sternly as possible.

"But I don't want to ask you for anything. I just wanted you to meet my mother…" Nandini didn't know what to say. She was not prepared for this.

"I hope your parents wouldn't have any objection, if you meet a foreigner's – mother!"

Robin asked. Nandini felt ashamed about her attitude. She shouldn't have acted so rudely!

"Of course not!" she managed to say with a smile.

Her Life Changed

Robin led the way to his mother and Nandini followed him. Behind them walked the two friends.

Robin stopped in front of a middle-aged couple. Nandini understood they were Robin's parents. The man was a Bengali, that Nandini could tell from his attire, but she was a bit confused about the lady. She was a white blonde but dressed up in a *saree*, just like any Bengali lady at the *Puja* Hall!

Robin introduced Nandini to his parents. "My father Mr. Subhashish Bannerjee and she is my mom Mrs. Sophiya Bannerjee and *ma*, she is the girl I was talking about. She hasn't told me her name yet…"

Nandini felt embarrassed again. "My name is Nandini… Nandini Roy and she is my friend Padma"

"*Nandini… Bhari mishti naam to* (Nandini…what a sweet name) " said Robin's mother.

Nandini smiled and bent down to touch her feet.

"*ekhane noy, Ma r saamne…* (Not here…in font of *Ma* Durga…) *ekdin bari eso bondhuke niye* (Come home some time with your friend)" she told Nandini and stopped her from touching her feet.

Nandini now remembered, "Bengalis didn't touch elder's feet during the five days celebration while Goddess Durga was there. Once they bade farewell to *Ma* Durga, they celebrated *Bijoya Dashami* (Victory of good over evil) when the young touched their elders' feet and elders blessed them."

How could she forget her own ritual and had to be reminded by someone not a Bengali!

However, Nandini liked Robin's mother very much. She was impressed by the way she dressed up and spoke Bengali!

"*Aapni ki sundor bangla bolen…* (You speak such beautiful Bengali)" Nandini said.

Robin was waiting for this moment. He took this opportunity to rise and shine. He continued, "My mother went to Shantiniketan as an exchange student for her Masters. That was where she met my dad. My dad was a Structural Engineer in one of the new buildings in Shantiniketan campus. They somehow met and after a couple of meetings, fell in love."

Nandini was listening very carefully. She looked at Robin's parents and smiled.

Robin's mother added, "That was like 30 years ago…*anek purono katha…* (Very old story)"

Robin continued, "After my mother finished her course, she returned to Melbourne. It became a long-distance relationship for them. My dad, I guess, didn't want to lose her, so he moved to Australia. They got married here. And then I was born – Rabindra Bannerjee. I became Robin or Rob, just to make it easy for everybody to pronounce my name. I look more like my mother, so somebody here mistook me to be a foreigner and rejected me."

Nandini was embarrassed. "I am really sorry about yesterday…" she said.

"That's okay…so ma…challenge *ta ami jitechi*… (I won the challenge) *Ekhon bakita tumi manage korbe.* (Now you will manage the rest) You promised me!"

Nandini was more impressed when she heard Robin speak Bangla, but she didn't quite understand what 'challenge' Robin was talking about!

"My mom always wanted a Bengali daughter-in-law. She said, she would find one through matrimony services but – it was not for me. I wanted to find one myself and fall in love!

That was the challenge!" Robin said.

"So did you fall in love?" Padma asked.

"Yes, I did…" Robin answered staring at Nandini.

Nandini now questioned, "You fell in love because I am a Bengali and you had to win the challenge?"

"Nope I fell in love first…when I first saw you at the restaurant…remember I came to serve you myself…that was when I thought you could be a Bengali! And then our tram ride…you ignored me, but I could hear a humming of Rabindra sangeet in my mind! If I correctly remember it was '*dariye acho tumi amar gaaner opaare*' (you are standing on the other side of the stream of my song)"

Puzzled and confused, Nandini sat down on a chair and asked Padma to get some water for her. Padma handed a bottle of water to her. She felt as if she was going to faint. She didn't expect Robin to recite the lyrics of a Tagore's song. She finished the bottle of water.

Robin had to complete his story. He said, "Yesterday when I met you here, I was double sure but then you just wouldn't listen to me, so I had to take my parents' help."

Robin's mother nodded her head and stopped Robin. "What's the hurry Rob? You both go out, *aage tomra katha bolo*, Nandini *k jigesh koro* if she is okay with it *tarpor amra Nandinir baba mar songe kotha bolbo*." (You both go out, get to know each other, ask Nandini if she is okay with it after that I will speak to her parents.)

It was very clear to Nandini now, what Robin was up to. She didn't know what to say, so she thought of taking leave. "I think we need to leave now Padma. We have to go a long way" Nandini got up ready to leave. She said bye to Robin's parents and promised to visit them during one of the weekends.

"Can we meet during this weekend for dinner…if you are free?" Robin asked.

"I think, I am free. You can call me," Nandini said.

"Sure, I will call you," Robin replied.

Nandini walked out of the Hall with Padma. The door closed behind her.

Robin was very happy. He was still staring at the closed door when his mother asked, "Have you got her mobile number?"

"Oops" exclaimed Robin, he ran out and Nandini was standing there, as if she was expecting that to happen.

She took out a piece of paper from her bag and wrote something, "Here you go."

Robin was ecstatic.

Nandini received Robin's call as soon as she reached home. Robin called to ask if they reached safely. Padma teased her. "Mr. Chef is deeply in love I don't think you will need to pay the next month's rent. You might move to his house before that!"

Their First Dinner Date

Robin knew exactly where he wanted to take Nandini, for their first date. Nandini was getting inquisitive about where they would go and texted Robin a couple of times. Robin kind of avoided that question. On a Friday, Robin called Nandini and asked her to meet him at the Crown Casino entrance at 5pm. (Crown is the biggest casino in the southern hemisphere and Robin wanted their first meeting to be grand).

Both were excited but Nandini was nervous. This was the first time ever she was going on a date and her parents had no clue about it.

Nandini wore a nice dress with a scarf. She reached Crown a few minutes early. It was going to be her first visit to the casino. She had seen a casino only in films. She was not sure if casino was the right place for their first date. It would have been better if Robin had decided on a quieter place! She thought.

He reached exactly on time. "Hello, good to see you Nandini. You look gorgeous today."

"Thank you!" said Nandini

Nandini started to walk towards the Crown Casino entrance, but Robin held her hand and stopped her.

"Wait – We are not going to the Casino," he said, "It's too noisy for our first date!"

"Oh! Where are we going then?" she asked.

Pointing to a tram line right in front of the Casino he replied, "We will take a tram ride, a special tram."

Nandini smiled. She liked the fact that Robin thought the same way as she did.

Holding her hand Robin continued, "Come with me." They walked about 500 meters away from the Casino, along the tram lines and reached the tram stop. Before Nandini could say a single word Robin said, "trust me you will love it."

Nandini smiled, she had started to trust Robin. After some time, there came her favourite red colour tram.

"We are taking that tram," Robin said. It looked like a tram, but it was a lot more than just a tram. "You first," he said.

As Nandini walked in, it all became clear to Nandini, they were going to have the best romantic dinner of their lifetime. They were going to have dinner in "The Colonial Tramcar Restaurant". (The burgundy colour tramcars are the first restaurants on wheels in the world. Diners enjoy an evening of exquisite dinner with chosen Australian wine).

They were assigned their table by a friendly waiter.

Nandini wasn't sure how to react. She pointed her finger out of the window at The Crown and said, "And I thought we were going to try our luck in there."

"We will one day, for sure" Robin replied. Nandini enjoyed every moment that evening. Robin impressed her and made his intentions clear.

He asked about Nandini's feelings. Nandini answered in short. "I will be honest with you. More than you, I fell in love with your mother!"

Robin laughed.

It was almost a month since Robin and Nandini talked and went for dinner during weekends. On the fourth weekend they finally visited the Crown Casino!

The entrance was very bright with thousands of blinking LED bulbs and the water fountain was dancing with joy to the background music. Everything was welcoming them in unison. The guard at the entrance smiled at them, "Welcome to Crown Casino." They held hands and walked through the magical the front entrance.

Robin asked, "Want to see what a million dollar looks like?" Nandini nodded with a yes.

"Close your eyes and don't let go of my hand."

They walked for about 200 meters and then Robin asked her to open her eyes.

"Wow!" she exclaimed. They were standing in front of a huge, floor to ceiling glass cylinder which contained a million one-dollar coins.

Nandini was awed with the opulence, action and clanking sound of falling coins in the "Coin tray" of the poker machines. This was her first time in a casino.

As they walked, Robin said, "You know, I have always been unlucky here. Never made any money in these poker machines. Shall we try our luck together?"

Nandini nodded "We can try. You never know." Robin tried his hand at the poker machines as Nandini watched. Very soon they realised that the poker machines were luckier, just like every other time before.

They spent some time looking around and walked into one of the restaurants. They had a romantic dinner. They were loving each other's company. Time just flew.

Love Blossomed

As time passed, they met over coffee, lunch and tea on numerous occasions. They were happy, comfortable and their bond was getting stronger with every time they met.

One Saturday morning they decided to meet up in front of the Flinders Street station in the city. As always, she arrived a bit early. She waited for Robin under the clocks at the main entrance, when she noticed big crowds at the Federation Square. Most of the crowd looked very Indian, wearing gorgeous Indian dresses.

Federation Square is the second most visited place in Melbourne, situated on the banks of river Yarra, comprising creative spaces for music, arts and major celebrations.

After a couple of minutes Robin arrived. "What's happening there?" asked Nandini.

Robin held her hand and said, "We are going there."

It was the "Indian Film Festival of Melbourne". Nandini was thrilled. She couldn't help but give Robin a big hug. She spotted a few renowned cinema artists from Bollywood.

Later that afternoon, Robin pulled out from his pockets, a couple of tickets to a Bollywood movie show. They watched the movie sitting close to each other holding hands. It was like a dream.

After the movie, they started to walk hand in hand along the Yarra River. Robin was very quiet. "He must be up to something today," Nandini thought.

Suddenly Robin stopped and looked into Nandini's eyes. He looked serious. Nandini wasn't sure how to react. In a very soft voice, he asked, "I have been waiting to ask you something, Nandini... We have been seeing each other for some time... and..."

"And what?" asked Nandini.

"And… I think we must end it all here," said Robin,

"What?" Nandini got the shock of her life.

"Yes…it's time we become husband and wife!" Robin gave her a naughty smile.

"Ohh…say that…you really scared me!" Nandini breathed a sigh of relief

Robin went down on his knees, held Nandini's hand and said, "Well I don't know how it's done. It's my first time," after a brief pause, he continued, "Will you marry me?"

Nandini pretended as if she was in deep thought, "I will, if you promise me that this is going to be your last time as well!"

Robin took a few seconds to understand what she meant, and then, "Well of course, that is what I meant. This is my first and last. Will you marry me Nandini?"

Nandini cried with joy. "Yes," she said nodding her head.

Robin stood up, took Nandini in his arms and they kissed. It was the sweetest feeling ever, that feeling of love and togetherness.

Nandini was very happy with the way her life was turning out in Melbourne. She was in love and Robin's parents had accepted her as their future daughter-in-law. Her working contract also got extended for another six months. But she had not yet told her parents about Robin. In fact, she didn't know how to tell them!

Like all parents, Nandini's parents always dreamt about their daughter getting married to the perfect life partner and living happily ever after. And the definition of a perfect partner in a middle-class Bengali family is a man with a good qualification, a good job and a fat salary, which according to them could be an engineer, a doctor or an Accountant!

Robin had none of the above credentials. He was training to be a chef and was working at a Michelin star restaurant as an apprentice.

Would Nandini's parents accept a Chef as their only son-in-law? Nandini was quite worried. She couldn't share that with Robin or his parents lest they get hurt.

One morning Nandini mentioned her worry to Padma. They had a long discussion and then Padma suggested that Nandini should invite her parents over, on the pretext of having a holiday in Australia and let them meet Robin and his parents.

Padma was sure just like Nandini, her parents would also happily fall in their trap!

They would also be mesmerized with Robin and his mother's Bengali in Australian accent!

Nandini quite liked Padma's idea. She also talked to Robin's mother about it. She agreed with the plan. She understood that although Nandini was an educated and independent girl, she still hesitated to talk to her parents about her love and marriage.

Robin's mother offered all help to Nandini on her venture.

Nandini somehow convinced her parents to visit her in Melbourne for a holiday.

It was late October, Nandini's parents were visiting her. They were excited and emotional. They were about to see their daughter after a long time. They had lots to talk about and brought lots of gifts for her too.

They finally landed at Tullamarine Airport. It was late at night and the flight from Singapore was long. They were tired but excited.

Nandini was waiting at the Arrival lounge. After clearing all formalities with immigration and customs, Nandini's parents walked out of the door. The door opened to a big hall with lots of people waiting. "Ma" shouted Nandini…

"There she is!" said her father.

Her mother hugged her as Nandini touched her feet. "*Kemon acho ma?* (How are you *ma*?)"

"*Tui bhalo achis to nandu*? (Hope you are good Nandu?)" asked her mother. Nandini nodded her head.

As the family met, Nandini's mother noticed a tall foreigner lady gorgeously dressed in a "silk *saree*" standing close to Nandini, smiling at them. Before Nandini could introduce her, she came to Nandini's mother and introduced herself in Bengali "*Namashkar, amar naam Sophia. Apnader dekhe khoob bhalo laglo*" (Namashkar, my name is Sophia, I am very happy to see you).

Nandini's parents greeted her in return.

Nandini's mother next spotted Robin. She looked him over from head to toe.

"*Amar chele Robin!*" (My son Robin!) Robin's mother said. Robin folded his hands with a bright smile to greet them. Nandini was standing still all this while. Looking at the changing expressions on her mother's face she started pushing the luggage trolley, "*Chalo ma anek door jete hobey…* (Let us go mother we have to go a long distance)" she said.

Tense Moments

Nandini was walking very fast. Everybody else was following her. Nandini's parents were quiet but could guess, there was something wrong!

All of them got into one car. Robin drove the car and Sophiya sat beside him. Nandini sat in the back seat with her parents. During the journey, Sophiya tried to have a conversation with Nandini's parents, all she got in reply was a "yes", "no" or a "hmm". Nandini tried to show them the city buildings, but her parents didn't look much interested. Robin and Sophiya dropped them at Nandini's house and went home.

Nandini tried very hard to make things easy and lower the tension. She had cooked rice and chicken curry which she thought her parents would be excited to try, but they were quiet.

Nandini felt very guilty. She should have told her parents about Robin. Her one secret had created a void between them that Nandini was trying very hard to fill by narrating all her achievements in Melbourne. Her parents were silent and didn't seem much impressed.

Nandini wanted to talk to her mother, but she said she was tired and wanted to go to bed. Nandini's father was already in bed. Nandini felt like crying but she controlled herself.

"They would meet Robin and his parents tomorrow and hopefully everything would be fine." She told herself.

The Families Met

Next morning, Nandini got up early and prepared tea for everybody. She broke the ice and told her parents the story of her journey with Robin. They listened to the story very patiently, and all they could do was smile. They felt much better. Even if what they guessed was correct, it was all about their daughter's happiness! They would have to accept.

"Ma, can you please wait for a few hours? it will all be clear!" she said.

"What do you mean?" asked her mother.

"We will all go out for lunch to a very nice place."

"Are we going to meet them today?"

"Yes *ma*, and you can ask them anything you want." Nandini answered.

After breakfast, Nandini called a Uber and the destination was "Sky High at Mt Dandenong" (Situated in the uppermost heights of Dandenong ranges amid cool ferny glades and native forest, Sky High is one of the tourist attractions in Melbourne. It has spectacular views of the city skyline and is known for good food, drinks and manicured lawns). It was a cool but sunny morning. After a decent drive along the mountains and greenery, they reached the parking entrance. They met Robin and his parents at the gate. They all greeted each other and headed for the restaurant where a big table for 6 was already booked by Robin's father. They sat next to a big glass window with a stunning view from the mountain top. The manicured gardens looked spectacular.

By now, Nandini's parents were 100% sure of what was to come. They were just waiting for the announcement.

Robin's dad started the conversation *"Amar naam Shubhashish Bannerjee, Ami Robin er baba* (My name is Shubhashish Bannerjee, I am Robin's dad.) *ar Sophiya r songey to apnader dekha hoyechey airport e* (you have met Sophiya already at the Airport) and he is my only son Robin!"

"Ami Arindam Roy, Nandini r baba ar o Aradhona, Nandini r ma. Apnader songe alaap kore khoob bhalo laglo… (I am Arindam Roy, Nandini's father and she is Aradhona, Nandini's mother. We are very happy to meet you.)"

"Same here. I think you can guess why we are here today. We are here to ask your Nandini's hand for my son Robin." Said Robin's father.

Nandini's parents had guessed it right! Without wasting any more time Nandini's mother asked her first question. "*Tumi ki koro Robin? mane…* (What do you do Robin? I mean…")

Nandini had dreaded this question since she had started dating Robin. She was worried about how her parents would take the answer, but Robin was prepared.

He said, "You mean my profession? Well, I am a trained chef, I completed my 3-year course and now I am an apprentice at a Michelin star restaurant in the CBD"

There was an eerie silence across the table. Nandini was waiting for her parents' reaction.

After a brief pause, Nandini's mother smiled and asked, "A Chef? Very interesting. So why did you choose to become a chef and not an engineer or a doctor? I am sorry but it just came to my mind"

It was a perfect opportunity to impress his to be mother-in-law. Robin took a couple of seconds to put his story together.

"I became a chef because I wanted to be one! Just like we need doctors and engineers we need Chefs too! Moreover, I think cooking is a process where science and art come together. We create a dish that not only tastes good, but also soothes our eyes. Getting the taste right is all about chemistry that involves acids, proteins and vitamins and the look is all about colour and shape and engineering! Good food makes people happy."

Nandini's mother looked impressed with Robin's answer.

"So, what's your plan for the future?" She asked her second question.

"My plan…is to have my own restaurant someday." Said Robin.

"Great. May God bless you and fulfil your wish!"

Nandini was surprised by her mother's response. She said to Robin, "you know my mother is an excellent cook! You can ask her if you want some tips on Bengali cuisine."

"Sure… I would love to," replied Robin.

Robin's father now turned towards Nandini's father, "*Sir apni kichu bolun!* (Sir, you say something!)"

"*Ami ar ki bolbo?* (What shall I say?) If my daughter is happy, I am happy. Only one question Robin… Are you ready to make a lifelong commitment?"

"Yes, Sir I am," Robin answered promptly.

"Good. Being the girl's father, today's treat should have been from my side but nevertheless, you will have to come to our house and give us a chance to serve you." He invited Robin's parents with folded hands.

Nandini's mother agreed with her husband and added, "Yes! And now that everything is fixed, we can have a little *aashirwaad* ceremony that day (A pre-wedding ceremony to bless the couple and announce the wedding officially to relatives and friends). I hope it is okay with you."

Robin's mother promptly answered, "Yes of course that would be lovely!"

The two families had a hearty time, they talked openly, shared all family stories.

They were comfortable and Nandini was the happiest girl in the world.

After the successful meeting, it was time to head back home. On the way back Nandini couldn't resist asking her parents, "*Baba* tell me frankly…you actually don't have any objection to this marriage or are you just agreeing to make me happy?

"No why should I have any objection?" her dad replied with a smile.

"Because Robin is a chef! I am sure you had wished for a better qualified son-in-law!'

"See Nandu, we as parents, prefer engineers or doctors or boys on government jobs to ensure our daughters have a secured life but, in my case, I have a daughter who is an engineer herself and is financially independent. So, you don't need a husband to give you security. I actually wished for more!"

"What do you mean *baba*?" asked Nandini.

"I wished for other qualities in my son-in-law like commitment, compassion, honesty and all those which make a good human being, who can be my daughter's best friend for life. And Robin has all these qualities!"

Nandini hugged her father. She had tears in her eyes.

"Moreover, the family is very good. The way Robin's mother has accepted her husband's culture and kept the family traditions alive is commendable. She knows about all the rituals to be done during a Bengali marriage!" Nandini's mother added. Her mother was kind of convinced that she couldn't have found a better husband for Nandini, herself.

Nandini now hugged her mother. She was very happy, but she felt guilty that she hid all these from her parents.

"I am sorry *ma* for keeping everything a secret. I was very scared. I had promised you that I wouldn't get involved with a foreigner."

"Shut up Nandu. Robin is more Bengali than you! And I won't tolerate anyone saying anything against my son-in-law! I hope I have made it clear!"

Nandini and her father burst out laughing.

Wedding Plan

Nandini's parents found an auspicious day in the very next week and invited Robin and his parents for the *ashirwaad* (engagement) ceremony.

Nandini's mother arranged everything with a lot of care. She decorated the house with flowers, put *alpona* (floor motifs done with colours and rice powder paste) at the entrance and planned an authentic Bengali menu for the occasion.

Nandini teased her mother. "*Ma* so much preparation for just a pre wedding ceremony *(aashirwaad)*? What will you do for my wedding?"

"You will have to wait to see that. I have also learnt to keep secrets." she said.

Nandini was hurt at her mother's response. She realized her mother had still not forgiven her. She decided to remain quiet.

Robin arrived with his parents well on time. They got gifts for everyone.

The ceremony started at the auspicious time. Nandini and Robin sat in two different rooms. First Robin's parents gave their blessings to Nandini. Robin's mother gifted her with a beautiful necklace set.

Next Nandini 's parents gave their blessings to Robin. They were happy but had tears in their eyes. Nandini's mother took off the gold chain she was wearing and gave it to Robin. Robin was a bit embarrassed whether to take it or not. At this Nandini's mother said, "Take it. It is my blessing. I would have come better prepared if I had a clue."

Robin and his parents loved the food. They highly appreciated Nandini's mother's culinary skills.

After the feast they sat down for a chitchat. Everyone was happy.

"I don't know, if I should say this or not..." started Nandini's mother and then she paused. Everyone waited for her to continue. Nandini got worried, her mother was unpredictable at times.

"I don't know if it is possible... Can we have Robin and Nandini married before we head back to Kolkata? May be a celebration with close friends and your relatives. I hope you can understand, being a daughter's mother, I am a bit worried."

Everybody was surprised and quiet. Nandini's father understood it was not possible in such a short time. Their return was in another two weeks. He tried to explain to Nandini's mother. "Aradhona, try to understand, planning a marriage ceremony takes time and..." Nandini's mother remained quiet She was waiting for Robin's parents to react.

Robin's father said, "The problem is we don't have enough time. This will be the first marriage in our family, and everybody would want to participate."

Robin's mother said, "I can understand your worries Mrs. Roy. We can have a small ceremony with close family and friends and get the marriage registered. What do you say Robin and Nandini?"

Robin nodded to say he agreed to the proposal. Nandini smiled and agreed too.

"Thank you, Mrs. Bannerjee. But the real Bengali Wedding will happen in Kolkata at our house following all rituals! And you will have to come over with your family and friends."

Robin's mother loved the idea and agreed happily but Robin's father got a bit worried. They had a big family and lots of friends. He said, "Most of my family live in and around Kolkata, getting my relatives wouldn't be a problem. But Sophiya's family is big, and they all live here. I think it will be a bit over our budget to get them all to Kolkata. I mean arranging their tickets and accommodation and everything else will be a bit expensive you know."

Robin's mother looked a bit annoyed with her husband. She said, "Shubho, you don't have to think everything in terms of money. I think my family will never miss this opportunity to witness a grand Bengali wedding and visit the city of joy!"

Nandini's father reassured him, "*Dada* (brother), you just have to get all of them to Kolkata. Rest all will be on me. Our traditional house has enough rooms to accommodate lots of guests. So, accommodation and food will not be a problem. Please give us an opportunity to be your host. Nandini is our only child, and we would like the celebration to be grand."

"Okay, agreed. But sir remember, you will have a large noisy Aussie crowd!" said Robin's father.

Nandini was quiet but Robin couldn't hold his emotions in any longer.

He shouted, "YES YES YES!" and everybody laughed.

A New Life Together

The wedding date was fixed for a Sunday, a couple of days before Nandini's parents had their flight.

Nandini's mother looked worried. Although she had asked for it, she didn't know how all the arrangements would be done in such a short time. The city was unknown to her. She didn't have a choice but to take help from Robin's family. His parents were happy to help. They took Nandini's parents to a few locations.

Nandini's parents decided on Sky-high at Dandenong, the same place that they had their first meeting, as the venue. A simple but authentic menu was decided for the guests. Robin's father talked to the pundit at the temple for performing a *havan* (A fire ritual performed on special occasions) and did the needful for registering the marriage.

On the wedding day, Robin and Nandini, after arriving at Sky-high went straight into a private room. They got dressed in their wedding attire and did some final touches. Robin was dressed in a typical Bengali *dhuti punjabi* (Bengali attire worn by the groom in a wedding). Nandini's dad helped Robin tie it up. Nandini was helped by her mother to dress like a bride. She wore a red silk *saree* (Indian dress draped around the body by Indian women). Her mother made a beautiful design on her forehead using sandalwood paste and put a *mukut* (tiara) which she made using flowers.

Robin and Nandini made the perfect couple and looked gorgeous. The wedding ceremony was held at the open gardens. They exchanged garlands and performed *havan* chanting the mantras recited by the pundit (the priest) in front of the fire. Robin put *sindoor* (red vermillion powder used by married women in India) on Nandini after the *havan*.

Robin's relatives and friends watched the ceremony and wished them well.

The wedding celebrant also arrived on time. All the legal proceedings were completed. Finally, Robin and Nandini were declared 'Husband and Wife'.

Everybody enjoyed a grand lunch at the Sky-high. Before they left, Nandini's parents invited them formally for the Final Wedding celebration at Kolkata. The wedding date would have to be decided after consulting a priest.

As per traditions, the bride moved to the groom's house after marriage. Robin's mother was okay with not following the ritual and asked Nandini to be with her parents till they left for Kolkata. But Nandini's mother didn't agree to it.

She was very strict though. She said, "A ritual is a ritual, and it cannot change according to our convenience. Nandini cannot stay back in her parents' house after marriage…she must follow her husband and go to her in-law's house. She now has new roles to play of being a wife and a daughter-in-law."

So Nandini's parents returned home with Nandini's friends and Nandini went to her in-law's house. There she was given a warm welcome. Robin's mother gifted her another set of jewellery and Robin gave her a diamond ring on white gold. Nandini loved it.

The next day Nandini went back to her parents to spend some time before they left for Kolkata. They just stayed at home and talked.

The following day Nandini's parents flew back to Kolkata. Nandini and her parents didn't feel bad at all. They were going to meet very soon in Kolkata for the mega wedding. In fact, Nandini's parents were happy to see their daughter settle down with Robin. They loved their son-in-law and the family. Nandini's dad slept well on the flight.

While they drove back from the airport, after dropping Nandini's parents, Robin suggested that Nandini should pack a few of her clothes. He wanted to go on a long drive next morning.

"Where are we going?" asked Nandini.

"I think we need some *us* time. We will go somewhere!!" replied Robin.

The next morning, they drove along the Great Ocean Road enjoying the sea and the sun. (Great Ocean Road is one of the best scenic drives along the south-eastern coast. It is a 242 km drive between Torquay and Allansford in Victoria). Nandini loved the surprises that Robin gave her. They had the best romantic time ever. They checked-into one of the sea facing luxury villas for a two-night stay. They just relaxed and chilled with each other. It was just them, cut off from the rest of the world.

The Unexpected Happened

Nandini's parents settled back in Kolkata after their eventful visit to Melbourne.

Without wasting any time, they started planning for the gala wedding celebration. There were festivities in the air. Everybody was very happy. It was going to be the first wedding in the family. Robin was the first Australian son-in-law in their family history.

Nandini's mother had already started shopping for the big occasion. Her mother would very often have a video chat with Nandini to show the purchases she made.

In Melbourne, everybody got busy with their daily life.

One day while chatting online Nandini's mother complained of chest pain.

Nandini was worried, "*Ma ki holo?* (Mother what happened?)"

Touching her chest, she replied "I have little pain here. I think I need some rest.

Nothing to worry."

Her father quietly walked in the room "What happened?"

"Nothing, I feel a bit uneasy. I need some rest," she said.

"OK *ma*, please take some rest. I will talk to you tomorrow," said Nandini.

Nandini's mother lay in bed.

After about a couple of hours Nandini received a call from her father. Her mother still had pain. Their family doctor had advised him to take her mother to the hospital emergency, without wasting any time.

"I have called an ambulance. I will call you back later." he said.

Nandini was worried and anxious. She couldn't wait for her father to call back. After waiting for a few minutes, she made a video call. Her mother was on the way to the hospital. She was in the ambulance, with her father by her side and an oxygen mask on her face.

Nandini was shocked to see her mother in that situation, but decided to stay positive

"*Ma chinta koro na* (mother, don't worry), you will be fine. You are going to the best hospital. Don't worry. Do you still have pain?"

Her mother removed her oxygen mask and replied in a soft voice, "I feel uneasy, not really pain. *Janina phire asbo ki na…ekta ashojjyo bytha buker kachhe* (Don't know if I will return home or not. It's a weird kind of pain)"

Nandini said, "Don't say that *ma*. You will be fine. We will visit Kolkata soon. You have to organise a big wedding for us." Her mother didn't say anything, she just smiled back.

As they reached hospital emergency, she was taken to the ICU. Doctors did everything necessary to stabilise her condition as they performed various tests on her. Everybody was stressed. Nandini wanted to fly back to Kolkata to be by her mother's side. Her father advised her not to.

Nandini's mother's prediction came true. She didn't make her way back home. She passed away late that night after a massive heart attack. She was a big fighter, but this time she couldn't win. The family was devastated.

During this whole time Robin and his family were always with Nandini. Nandini's father was heartbroken. He was relieved though that Nandini had found a new family, a family of her own and was settled.

Her mother's body was cremated by her father. Nandini felt helpless and watched all the rites being performed over video calls. She asked Robin to book her tickets to Kolkata. Robin didn't want to let Nandini travel the distance by herself. He decided to travel with her and be there for the *Shradhha* ceremony (a prayer ceremony held for the departed soul on the 13th day from the date of death).

Nandini and Robin had already started planning for their visit to Kolkata but never realized it would be so soon and that too for such a sad occasion.

Robin organised the ticket in a hurry. On the day of travel, Robin's dad dropped them at the Tullamarine Airport.

They reached Kolkata after a stopover in Singapore.

Chapter 3

Kolkata - The City of Joy

"*This is where I started my journey two years ago,*" Nandini whispered to Robin, standing outside the Airport at Kolkata.

For the first time in this whole episode Robin had tears in his eyes.

Nandini was feeling much "lighter" after meeting her dad and crying her heart out. All the emotions that she had held in her heart for the past few days, were finally out.

She was smiling. "Seems like it was only yesterday, that I left this place," she said.

Robin noticed a change in Nandini – Kolkata was successful in making Nandini smile. She had stopped smiling since her mother had passed away.

"Let's go." Nandini's dad said holding her hand and started walking to the carpark. She was still his little girl. Robin just followed them.

As they walked towards their car, a man came running towards Nandini and said,

"*Kemon acho didi? Dekho ki hoye gelo? Bhogoban er ichchey.* (How are you sister? See what happened… Everything happens according to god's wish!?)"

"*Haan ki ar bolbo? Ami bhalo, tumi bhalo acho to?* (What can I say? I am fine. Hope you are well too?)" Replied Nandini.

He opened the car door and asked Robin and Nandini to sit. He then put all the luggage in the car boot. They settled inside the car, Nandini looked at Robin and said, "Ram kaka has been with us for the last 25 years now. He used to take me to school."

On the way home, Robin saw a couple of Kolkata trams moving at a gentle pace on the tram tracks running parallel to the roads. "They look so good! Now I know why you love the city circle tram-rides so much!" Robin said looking at a tram outside. Nandini smiled.

Welcome at Nandini's House

The car rolled through the narrow streets of Kolkata and finally stopped in front of an old house with traditional Bengali architecture and character. There was a sudden commotion at the house entrance, somebody shouted "*Eshe gechey* (They have come)."

A couple of young boys came running and stood around the car. One of them opened the car doors. Nandini's dad got out first and started walking. Robin and Nandini got out of the car and followed him. Everyone was silent. They walked through a narrow passage that led to the central hall of the house. The ladies and children were standing on both sides welcoming them with teary eyes. Many of the ladies were sobbing.

Many of the young kids, oblivious to what had happened, were all happy with sparkles in their eyes. For them it was a happy occasion. Nandini was coming home after a long time. They were hoping that Nandini would have got gifts for them. The men were busy doing crowd control and making way for them on the walkway. There were mixed emotions around.

Ideally, the first visit by a son-in-law would be a reason for celebration, but not for them. There were lots of people around them, Nandini was still looking around for that someone, somewhere deep inside she knew that she wasn't going to find her.

Nandini walked up to one of the aunties standing outside the kitchen and Robin followed. She cried as she hugged her aunty.

"*Ki bolbo kakima, maer jaoar khoob tara, shesh dekhar o somoi dilo na* (Aunty, what shall I say, *ma* was in a hurry to go, she didn't even give me time to see her one last time)"

"*Kadis na nandu, ma dukhkho pabe* (don't cry Nandu, your mother will be sad)." Aunty consoled Nandini. After a brief pause, she continued "*tora ja ektu rest korey ney. Amra ektu porey aschi tor ghorey.* (You get some rest. We will come to your room a little later.)"

Nandini's father tried to act normal and kept a straight face.

He looked at Robin and said, "This is our ancestral home, 150 years old."

"Yes, all the furniture and the pictures in the house are hundreds of years old. You know Robin every item in the house has a story. *Baba* will tell you." Nandini added.

Robin was overwhelmed. He didn't know how to react. He just nodded.

Nandini walked into her parent's room. Robin followed. One of the walls had quite a few pictures of the family. Right in the middle, was a big portrait of her mother with a garland around it. Nandini went and touched her mother's photo, trying to get that connection probably. "Why did you have to go so early *ma*?" she whispered. Tears rolled down her cheeks. She started crying uncontrollably. Robin held her hand firmly.

Nandini's father waited for Nandini to calm down a bit and said, "She probably knew she had to go…that's why she was in a hurry to get you married! Go to your room and take some rest. Take care of Robin. I will see you later in the afternoon."

As they walked along the corridor, Robin heard a weird welcoming voice, he was not sure what it was! He looked around but couldn't see anyone. He looked at Nandini, he wanted to ask what this voice was about!

Nandini smiled and said, "Come I will introduce you to my sister" and took Robin to the other side of the open corridor. There hung a large cage with a green parrot inside!

"She is Tiya. My mother's pet parrot. She loved her as much as she loved me. She was four when I was born. So Tiya is kind of my elder sister."

Tiya repeated "Welcome. How are you?"

Robin smiled back and said, "Thank you Tiya, we are fine."

Right next to the cage was a small *puja* (prayer) room. Every morning, Nandini's mother, after her bath, would come to the room to perform her puja. Tiya would eagerly wait till her puja was done. Tiya would then get her treat for being a good girl, her favourite seeds, and water.

Nandini continued, "You know everyone said *ma* and Tiya had a soul connection. *Ma* understood every move of Tiya's. Many a time, *ma* opened the cage and asked her to fly away but she didn't. I am sure Tiya must be missing *ma* badly."

Nandini's room was on the first floor, at the end of the long corridor. Robin followed Nandini to her room. Their room was freshly painted and had traditional hand carved furniture. The walls were adorned with some of the embroidery work done by her mother.

"Wow, this is amazing. Better than a five-star hotel!" Said Robin.

Nandini smiled. "My mother was very good at stitching," she said looking at one of the wall hangings. All the furniture is more than a hundred years old."

They had a quick shower and relaxed. Robin turned on the television to have some Kolkata news while Nandini lay in bed. The girl from the kitchen got them tea and biscuits on a tray.

While they were having their tea, Robin could hear people talking. There was a gathering outside their room. Robin looked at Nandini. She knew exactly what it was!

She opened the door and asked everybody to come in.

"Everyone is waiting to meet you." She said.

One by one, Nandini quickly introduced her cousins, uncles and aunts to Robin.

After everybody went out Robin said, "You have quite a big family." He was exhausted.

"You got scared? don't worry, nobody will interfere in our affairs."

"I am not worried. It's okay." He replied with a smile.

Next two days they relaxed, and Robin was loving the daily routine. He didn't have to do anything in the house. Food was served, all clothes washed, chauffeur driven car at his disposal – what else could a Bengali Prince ask for! Robin, on a couple of occasions, accompanied his father-in-law to the shops for buying things for the shraddha ceremony.

Nandini met with all her friends and relatives. Everybody visited her to offer their condolences.

Every morning they would wake up with the "Good morning, Breakfast is ready" message by Tiya and invariably hear Tiya welcome everybody entering the house.

The Hidden Memories

Nandini was talking to her father one morning. She got emotional looking at her mother's old cupboard. "You know *baba*, as a child I always wanted to see what was inside. *Ma* would sometimes show me some things and keep it back!"

Her father gave her the keys and said, "Your mother always kept that locked. Now you have the keys, go ahead! I am sure there are lots of secrets in there."

As she opened the cupboard her father continued, "Your mother never allowed anyone to touch her cupboard, not even me. In case you need something, take it. She will be happy to see her daughter using her things, wherever she is!"

Nandini very carefully took out things that hadn't been touched for ages. She found her mother's *sarees*, her old picture album, jewellery for daily use, some old books and magazines that her mother had preserved. At the bottom of the pile was a brown paper wrapped *saree* and on top it said, "my wedding *saree*."

Nandini was in tears and shouted, "*Baba*, come and have a look at what I found!"

Her dad came running, saw the *saree* and said in an emotional tone, "Your mother wanted to give it to you on your wedding day, but…" he was choking as he said that. Nandini smiled with teary eyes.

She put everything back in the cupboard and decided to continue later.

The Shraddha Ceremony

(Condolence meeting)

The next day, Nandini woke up early in the morning. It was the thirteenth day after her mother had passed away. She saw there was a big gathering in the central courtyard.

Lots of activities were happening.

She went up to her father and asked, "What's happening *baba*? Today is ma's shraddha! It's looking like a celebration!"

"Yes…today is the day to show our love and respect to her for all that she has done for us. We will make her favourite dishes and pray to God for her onward journey."

"Shall I come and help?"

"No there are enough people to do all the work. You can just go and monitor them. Your mother will like it if she is watching you from somewhere. You are her only child!"

Nandini had a shower. She wore one of her mother's *sarees*. She stood next to the window as she combed her hair and watched everything.

A couple of professional chefs were organising everything. Traditionally, in Bengali events, professional chefs are brought in-house, and all dishes are cooked in a central place, typically an open courtyard. They had made two makeshift "open-fire cook tops" with brick and mud. One for making the main meals like rice, vegetables etc. and the other for making desserts.

On the side of the courtyard, a place for *havan* (to light a fire and perform puja and prayers) was made. Just next to it stood a *pandal* (a temporary hall created with bamboo and large pieces of cloth made for holding events with large gathering) where people would come and sit and pray for the departed soul. There was also a separate eating area where tables and chairs were arranged in rows.

Nandini's mother had planned on having her wedding celebration in the same courtyard. She had told Nandini her plans. But unfortunately, the situation was very different now.

"Robin, I have kept your clothes outside on the table. Have a shower, wear them, and please come down. I am going down," said Nandini. She walked down the stairs to the courtyard. There was a group of ladies, cutting vegetable and grinding spices.

Nandini went straight to the *puja* (prayer) room. Her mother's photograph was kept there. She picked it up and cleaned it. A small bowl of sandal paste was kept there.

She decorated her mother's photograph with beautiful motifs with sandal paste just like her mother did on her wedding day! She also put *alpona* (designs made with rice powder) on the floor in front of her photograph.

Around mid-day, the *havan* fire was lit. The priests started chanting mantras. Nandini and Robin sat with the priests. Nandini was asked to repeat the mantras and do a few rituals. Nandini was crying all throughout. The priest explained to her, "Don't cry so much dear. Your tears will cause more pain to your mother's soul. Let it be free! Pray that she gets *moksha* (liberation from the cycle of birth and death)."

Nandini tried to remain calm and control her emotions. After the *havan* was over, she distributed alms to the poor.

Guests started pouring in. They prayed for the departed soul and the family's wellbeing. They met the newly-wed couple and blessed them. They were feeling sorry for them. All the events got over by late afternoon.

The next few days Nandini remained at home. It was hard to come to terms with the fact that her mother was no more. Her father asked her to go out and show places around Kolkata to Robin, but Nandini didn't want to do anything. Robin understood and supported her.

One day, a few of her close friends visited her. They wanted to go on a picnic near the river. Nandini straight away refused.

"Do you think aunty would be happy to see you sad all the time? Be ready tomorrow morning. We will pick you up. No excuses please." Said one of her friends.

Nandini was hesitant at first but agreed after her father stepped in.

Phool Sojja

(Honeymoon)

Next morning Nandini's friends turned up, six of them and they all got in a big van. "Where are we going?" Asked Nandini.

"A surprise for you," replied her friend.

They reached the banks of *Ganga* (river) and right in front was a big boat, beautifully decorated for a special occasion. Nandini and Robin were the first ones to board.

Nandini noticed a big heap of flowers, white and red and lots of local produce.

The boat started cruising at a very gentle pace as the waves splashed on the sides of boat.

Nandini was confused, but before she said anything, her friend announced, "We will spend the next 24 hours together and Nandini and Robin you will have the best time ever – Bengali style"

They all settled in the sitting area of the boat. They were served an elaborate lunch.

They told Robin about their school and college days and asked about his love story. They were having a great time. At around 3 pm the boat stopped at the bank and two local men boarded the boat. Unaware of what was planned, Nandini got a bit worried. The two guys entered in one of the rooms and closed the door. Nandini tried to ask one of the friends, but she was told not to worry.

As the sun set and it got dark, Nandini was called inside one of the rooms. One of her friends took out a big brown packet and pulled out her mother's wedding *saree* that Nandini had found in her mother's cupboard. They also got a *dhuti punjabi* (traditional Bengali dress for men) for Robin. Her friend said, "Tonight is the night – your *phoolsajya* (first night as husband and wife), you and Robin get ready and come out." Nandini was lost for words. She smiled with teary eyes. Nandini and Robin, with their friends' help dressed up in the attires given to them.

As they walked out of the room Nandini looked at Robin and said, "Wow, you look like a Bengali film hero." One of her friend's agreed, "Yes, you look very handsome in that *dhuti punjabi.*"

Robin smiled, "Thank you. You look gorgeous in your red *saree.*" Turning towards the friends he continued "What do you think guys?"

Everybody agreed that they looked awesome, and they were going to have the best night ever.

The dinner was being cooked on the boat with all local ingredients, by a cook hired by them. Robin was loving all the smell of spicy food being cooked on the deck. He took a deep breath to smell the spices. He even sneaked out to check on the dishes being prepared.

"*AJker menu ki* (What's today's menu?) he asked the chef. "*Rui macher kalia, kosha mangsho, aloo kopir jhol, tomato chatni ar rosogolla* (Rohu fish preparation, dry mutton curry, potato and cauliflower, tomato chutney and rosogolla) replied the chef.

"*Darun gondho beriyeche. Ki moshla dichcho?* (Smells very nice, what spices are you using?)"

"*Oi gota groom mosla, panchphoran, ada, rosun, ar khejur porbe chatni tey* (whole garam masala, five spices, ginger, garlic and dates with the tomato chutney.)" Replied the chef.

Robin then quietly joined the crowd in the sitting area.

Nandini's friends sang a series of romantic Bengali songs while having dinner on the boat. The food was delicious. After a while one of the friends said "Forget about us now Nandini… we don't exist for you here. It's all about just the two of you. Enjoy your night! That's your room." They pointed towards a room where the two men had been working earlier.

Nandini was a bit shy, and Robin was uncomfortable. They walked into the room and what they saw was amazing! Their bed was beautifully decorated with white *Rajnigandha* (tuberose – sweet smelling flower used in typical Bengali weddings) and big red roses. The smell of rajnigandha and rose filled the room.

Robin forgot that their friends were outside the room, he took Nandini in his arms and kissed her passionately. It was a special night for them. They enjoyed every moment, as if it was their first night together. They both experienced the best feeling of togetherness – silent, passionate, and memorable. Robin whispered, "I am going to remember this for the rest of my life."

Next morning, Robin walked out of the room and said, "A big thank you to all of you. I had the best time of my life!"

One of the friends replied, "That was the whole idea!" Then she whispered in Nandini's ear, "In fact this was your mother's idea Nandini. She had called us and discussed the plan in detail." Nandini was touched. She couldn't hold back her tears.

They were about to end the boat experience after their breakfast. Everybody wanted to stay a bit longer, but Nandini wanted to go back home. She was worried for her *baba*. She wanted to spend the rest of her time with him, as long as she was here.

The Sensational Discovery

Robin and Nandini's stay in Kolkata was about to end in a few days.

Nandini opened her mother's cupboard. She wanted to carry back a few of her things with her as memory. Her mother's cupboard was like a Pandora's box. On the top shelf Nandini found her baby dresses, hand stitched frocks that her mother had made, many of her dolls that she used to play with, her old school annual reports and the drawings that she made while in school. Her mother had preserved all the memories of Nandini, as if she wanted to present it back to her one day. The memories were priceless.

The middle shelf had all her *sarees* and jewellery and different photographs.

At the bottom shelf, Nandini found a thick notebook named "***Panchforon*** (Five Spices) – By Sreelekha". It had beautiful pictures and illustrations of different kinds of dishes and interior designs of what looked like a restaurant. It also contained recipes of different cuisines, Plans of kitchen and seating arrangements and designs of menu cards. There was also a financial plan on the last page!

Nandini was surprised. She knew that her mother took extra interest in cooking. She had taken part in some of the local food competitions during *Durga Puja* and won a couple of awards. But this notebook was like a mystery. It belonged to some Sreelekha but the handwriting was her mother's.

Nandini didn't talk to anybody about it but couldn't stop thinking. One question kept popping up in her mind "Who was Sreelekha and what was her relationship with her mother?"

At night she showed the notebook to Robin. The illustrations looked awesome. Robin thought of it more like a project plan.

Next morning as they were having their tea, Nandini asked her father "*Baba*, who is Sreelekha?"

Her dad was a bit puzzled and asked, "Why do you ask that?"

Nandini then got the notebook. "I found this in ma's cupboard. Who is Sreelekha?"

Her dad smiled and said "That's a long story. Wait, I will get something for you," and he went back to his room and came back with a file and gave it to Nandini.

Nandini opened the file and was surprised to see cut-outs of pages from Bengali magazines that were decades old, carefully filed. The pages contained articles titled "*Sreelekha's Rannaghor* (kitchen)."

The pages contained recipes and excellent discussion on modern Bengali cuisine. It also featured feedback from the readers.

Nandini went through a few of the pages and exclaimed, "Wow – but *baba*, who is Sreelekha?"

There was silence in the room, after a brief pause Nandini's father said, "Your mother! This column was written by her."

Nandini got a shock, "What are you saying *ma* used to write! But why Sreelekha?"

Nandini's father started the story, "It all started one day when a friend of mine, who was working for a publisher had come home for dinner. He was impressed by your mother's cooking and casually asked her to write an article on cooking. Ours was a conservative family and it was not easy for your mother to get permission to work, that too write for a magazine on cooking! So, she refused my friend."

"But *baba*, how come you let me work?" Nandini asked.

"Times have changed now. Girls can do everything now."

"Thank God for that!"

Her dad continued, "After a year or so my friend sent me a magazine and asked me to read and comment on their regular column *Sreelekha's Rannaghor* (kitchen)! I loved it very much. My friend then disclosed that it was written by your mother. Your mother didn't want to break the family tradition and defame her professor husband, so she used an alias – Sreelekha. I promised my friend that I wouldn't talk to your mother about it. Thereafter, I made sure I got a copy of the magazine every month. I read the articles and cut out the relevant pages for my personal collection. There you have the collection in your hand"

"Did you both hide it from each other?" asked Nandini.

"Yes! I was scared that she might stop writing but you know what?" her dad asked,

"What?" asked Nandini,

"I used to comment regularly. You will see many comments from a Polly Dutta…" said her dad.

Nandini went through the pages and said, "Yes, Polly Dutta!"

"That was me… I kept on communicating with your mother, on a regular basis using my new alias." Her dad laughed.

"Hmm…ma was very creative with food. But did you know about this? She also wanted to open up her own restaurant?" Nandini said, holding the notebook with the restaurant plan.

"Not really… I never saw this before, but she used to often say if given a chance she would have her own restaurant"

"Why didn't you help her open up one?" she asked.

"It is not easy Nandu…no one ever did any business in our family…and I didn't like the idea that your mother would be cooking the whole day for others. Frankly speaking, I also thought it would hurt my reputation…but now I feel I should have encouraged her or at least shared her dream…she has gone with an unfulfilled desire…" her dad replied with teary eyes.

"Hmm, now I understand why *ma* was so thrilled when Robin said he wanted to have a restaurant of his own!" Nandini remembered fondly.

Her dad nodded and said, "Yes and you know what she told me when we were flying back?"

"What?"

"She said, you never listened to me, but God has sent me a partner in the form of my son-in-law. My dream will come true now!"

Nandini and her father remained quiet for some time.

"Can I take this with me *baba*?" holding the notebook in her hand, Nandini asked.

"Of course, you can but can I have a copy of this? I will at least go through them now…"

That night Nandini couldn't sleep. She kept on thinking about her mother. While still dark, she got up and went out to the balcony.

Seeing her from the other side of the corridor, Tiya shouted, "Good morning. Breakfast is ready." Nandini scolded Tiya, "Shhhh… It's not morning yet Tiya. Stop shouting."

Tiya probably understood. She became quiet but by then Robin had woken up. He came out and stood next to her.

"What happened?" asked he.

"Nothing… Just couldn't sleep," Nandini said.

"Okay let's sit here and talk. You will feel better," suggested Robin.

Both sat on the chairs kept outside their room. Robin was holding Nandini's hand.

"Since I found ma's book, I have been thinking… *Ma* sacrificed her own wishes and dreams to fulfil mine and *baba's*."

Robin nodded his head. "She was a great wife and a mother!"

Nandini turned to Robin, "I want to make her dream true. Will you help me, Robin?"

"Sure, my love." Robin answered.

"You said you wanted to open your own restaurant. Can we open it now?" Nandini asked with a sparkle in her eyes

"Now? In the middle of the night?" Robin joked.

"I mean, in the near future?" Nandini asked again.

"Nandini, there are so many things that we will have to think about. I need more experience and contacts before I start my own restaurant! We will have to discuss it with people from different areas, which we can do once we get back to Melbourne."

"Hun… I understand it is difficult…but it is not impossible!" She tried to motivate Robin.

"Yes of course, nothing is impossible if you work hard for it."

Nandini felt happy to see that Robin at least agreed to try.

"Then promise me you will start the project as soon as possible and I promise to help in every possible way. I can't let her go with an unfulfilled wish! Robin, just think it this way, by helping me fulfil my mother's dream, you will also make your dreams come true."

Robin smiled, "You've got a point!"

Back to Australia

Nandini and Robin returned to Australia. Nandini felt sad and cried while leaving her father alone in Kolkata, but her father calmed his little girl. He promised to visit her in a few months.

Robin's parents were happy to have them back home. Robin shared his experiences with them. Most notable was his experience when they first arrived at Nandini's house and their unique *Phoolsajya* on the boat.

Special mention was of course, "Tiya the parrot."

Nandini and Robin soon got busy in their daily routine, but Nandini didn't forget about her mother's dream. She read her notebook many times. Then one weekend after dinner, she mentioned it to Robin. "Did you talk to anybody about opening your restaurant?" she asked hesitatingly.

"Yes, I did," Robin said, while looking at his mobile.

"You did?" Nandini was thrilled. "And I thought you had forgotten!"

Robin smiled, "How could I…because your mother's dream is my dream too! But our dreams would have to change a bit considering the business aspect of the project. Most of the people that I talked to felt that we should have an Indian restaurant, rather than a Bengali restaurant!

"That's good enough. Bengali dishes will be a part of the menu." Nandini understood.

"Brilliant idea Robin…" Nandini was very excited.

"But it requires a lot of money. I will have to talk to Dad about it."

Beginning of a New Journey

One Sunday morning after breakfast Robin shared with his parents Nandini's mother's passion and showed them her notebook.

Robin's mother said, "The way she planned her daughter's marriage without any preparation on a foreign land, I could easily tell that she was a lady of great calibre!"

Robin's father said, "This looks like a proper project plan."

Robin continued, "I have been thinking about my own restaurant for some time now. I think this is a good starting point. What do you think dad?" asked Robin.

Rob's dad nodded his head in agreement and said, "Everything else is fine but the finance will be difficult. I suggest work for a bit longer maybe and save some more money. You are still young. There is enough time to have your own restaurant. On the contrary, you can take some risk now, but once you have a family, it will be difficult."

"Dad you are confusing me now…" Robin said. His dad smiled at him and avoided any further conversation.

"Robin, you have to take the decision, considering the resources you have. After all it's your life!" his father ended the conversation.

Robin made his decision. He would have his own Indian restaurant. He met a few people who suggested he start by applying for bank loans.

Nandini also worked seriously on the project. She designed a smart logo and a menu card for Robin's restaurant. She just made a few changes in her mother's designs and made it more contemporary. She showed them to Robin, and he quite loved it.

They were going ahead with their project, when one morning Nandini fell sick. She threw up a couple of times during the day. Robin and his dad were worried, but his mom was not. She probably knew what was coming! Robin called up the doctor. The doctor advised that Nandini should take rest and not go to work. It could be because of all the hectic travel and busy schedule during their travel to India. They got an appointment for a few days later.

Nandini took rest but continued having the morning sickness. Robin was worried. "Don't worry Robin, its normal, just spend time with her whenever you can, she needs your attention." said Robin's mother while serving breakfast.

Robin thought of taking off from work, but his mother said, "I am here at home, I will look after her, you be happy and go to work."

Robin's mother looked after Nandini well. She got her favourite rice bubbles, made fresh orange juice for her, simple Bengali meals and took care of her the same way Nandini's mother used to do. Nandini felt grateful to her.

The Soul Connection

It was a Thursday. Nandini had an appointment with the doctor. The alarm clock rang at 6.30 am as every day. Robin woke up but was surprised to not see Nandini beside him in bed. He looked out of the window and saw Nandini sitting outside in their front garden. She was in deep thought. Robin got worried. Nandini was not able to come out of her grief and that was affecting her health.

Robin called her and she came inside.

"What happened?" asked Robin,

"Nothing… I am fine," replied Nandini and went to the bathroom to get ready. They had their breakfast and left for the doctor's clinic.

As they waited for their turn at the doctor's clinic, Robin asked Nandini, "What were you doing outside in the garden this morning?"

"Nothing…just getting some fresh air," she replied.

It was their turn. The doctor listened to Nandini and suggested that they should do a pregnancy test and guess what, the test was positive! Rob's face lit up with joy and so did Nandini's. The doctor checked Nandini and advised Robin to look after her and make sure she had good food and was happy.

As they drove back home from the clinic, Robin noticed Nandini was lost in her thoughts. He said, "Is something bothering you…are you not happy with the way our life is going at the moment?"

"I am very happy Robin," said Nandini, "and now even happier because my mother is coming to me!"

"What do you mean?" asked Robin.

"Last night I had a dream. My mom and I were walking hand in hand in a garden, but in my dream, I was the mother, and she was my daughter. I was very happy to see her. I hugged her and showered my love on her. Suddenly she left my hand and started running. I started running after her. And then I woke up. They say all the early morning dreams always come true. I could not sleep after that, so I went out and sat in the garden."

"So, you think we are going to have a daughter?" asked Robin,

"Yes, my mother is coming." She felt at peace

They came home and shared the news of Nandini's pregnancy with both parents.

Robin's parents were happy and so was Nandini's father. Robin observed that Nandini felt much better after the dream. She was happier and more active.

One Sunday morning, while having breakfast, Robin's father asked, "Any news on your restaurant plans Rob?"

"No, you were right dad, the main issue is the finance. I have applied for loan at a couple of banks, let's see. But looking at the present scenario, I think we have to scrap the restaurant idea for the time being. We can take it up once our life settles down a bit." He said and looked at Nandini. She didn't like it but didn't make any comment.

Robin's dad agreed, "yes, going through the nine months of pregnancy and becoming parents is a big project in itself. I think you both shouldn't stress too much. You can start the project once the baby is born. Sophiya, what do you think?"

Robin's mother agreed. Turning towards Nandini, she said, "I think dad is right. The restaurant can become your second baby."

Nandini was disheartened but she agreed that the restaurant could wait till the baby was born.

Time passed. Nandini was in her sixth month of pregnancy. One evening she felt quite uneasy. They went to the doctor; her blood pressure was on the higher side. The doctor advised her not to work and to rest at home. She needed to take rest and relax her mind. The doctor asked Robin to keep her busy with small bits of housework and not think or worry too much about anything.

Robin understood the reason for Nandini's stress. The restaurant project was postponed and that was not what she wanted.

Robin had a plan in mind. Next morning, he opened the project file and called Nandini. "It seems you have stopped working on my project. We have a lot of work Nandini. We haven't yet thought of a name for my restaurant. Suppose my loan goes through tomorrow, how will we manage?" he said.

"But I thought we had scrapped the project for now!" Nandini said.

"Yes, but in another few months our baby will be here. You will get very busy. Use the time, you have now! Do some research on the dishes and the promotional offers that restaurants give! Plan the décor and the walls…" Robin went on.

"But your mom and dad may not like it." Said Nandini

"Don't tell them…simple!" Robin solved her problem. Nandini looked very happy.

The next couple of days, she did a lot of online research but couldn't get anything interesting. She missed her mother very much.

In all her crisis in life, Nandini had always taken her mother's advice.

After dinner, she walked into her room and stood in front of her mother's photo. "*Ma* please help me," she whispered to herself. She was tired. She then lay on the bed flipping the pages of her mother's file. That night she again had a dream. She and her mother were in the spice market of Barabazaar (a famous wholesale market) in Kolkata. Her *ma* was buying different kinds of spices for Robin. Nandini didn't like the idea. "Who gives spices to her son-in-law?" she thought. Her mother selected exotic spices, which were all native Australian! Nandini's mother asked the shopkeeper to gift wrap the boxes. She then handed them over to Nandini. She started walking and Nandini followed her. Nandini was tired carrying so many boxes, so she stopped to rest a while. She turned to look for her mother, but she was nowhere! Nandini got scared. She called out "*Ma, ma* where are you?"

Robin walked into the room, held her hand and asked, "Are you ok? What happened?" Nandini realized it was only a dream.

"Yes, I am fine." She replied.

That whole day Nandini kept thinking about the dream. Was there any message in the dream or was it because she was flipping through the pages of the file while she fell asleep? Or was it because she searched for different kinds of dishes on google before going to bed? But why would her mother shop for Australian spices in Kolkata to gift Robin? She thought hard but couldn't figure it out!

After Robin came home from work, Nandini shared the dream with him.

"I think there is a message in the dream. Your *ma* is suggesting that we be a bit creative. She wants us to open a restaurant that is different – a fusion restaurant maybe." Robin said with conviction.

"I don't understand what you are saying." Said a confused Nandini.

"You won't because you don't understand culinary art. How I wish my mom in law was by my side today!"

"Robin please tell me what exactly you are saying?" Nandini asked.

"I think your mother wants us to have a restaurant where there will be a fusion of Bengali and Australian tastes. May be Bengali recipes cooked with aboriginal spices or vice versa…brilliant, isn't it?" said Robin quite satisfied with his comprehension of the dream.

"Yes, but then that will require a lot of experimenting with the dishes!" Nandini exclaimed.

"The idea is unique. I have decided. Our restaurant will be a fusion restaurant! Thank you, mom-in-law. Love you!" Robin said to Nandini's mother's photograph kept on her table.

Robin decided to start experimenting with dishes at home on the weekends.

On the weekend Robin quietly walked into the kitchen and asked his mother, "Mom can I do some cooking today? I want to try some new dishes."

"What are you going to cook? Can we have it for dinner?" asked Rob's mother.

"Oh yes but it's fusion cooking. Dad may not like it." Robin joked.

"What do you mean I will not like it?" shouted his dad.

Just then Nandini walked into the kitchen. Robin's mother said, "Rob is making some fusion dish for dinner. Come let's watch TV."

"Ma, let Nandini help me a bit. Doctor has asked me to keep her busy." Robin said.

Robin's mother agreed but his father got suspicious. "I hope you are not trying to fool us, Rob. Is your fusion cooking for the restaurant? I thought we had agreed to hold the restaurant plans till the baby was born?" he asked.

Robin agreed reluctantly. "Yes dad, we are just experimenting with dishes and taking our plans further and nothing more"

"That's good. I just want to say Nandini's blood pressure is high. She shouldn't take any kind of stress. Believe me, it will be very difficult to set up the restaurant in the current situation." Robin's father concluded.

Nandini understood well that Robin's parents cared for her and said everything for her good, but she couldn't forget her dreams and the message she got from her mother. Somehow, she had a feeling that her mother was in a hurry for this restaurant to be established.

Chapter 4

The Restaurant

The next few weeks Nandini and Robin worked quietly on the new recipes.

Robin talked to some of his chef friends with aboriginal background who had experience in cooking with native spices. He spent a few days to finalise the list of dishes to be served. He replaced the Indian spices with local spices for the dishes. Now came the biggest challenge – taste. Robin created and modified some of Nandini's mother's Bengali recipes using local ingredients and native spices. After a couple of repeated trials, the dishes took shape. The food tasted delicious and looked exactly as he had visualised. Robin then invited family and friends for a blind tasting. Robin's dad didn't like them going ahead with the restaurant in a hurried way, but he loved the food. So, did everybody else. The taste and texture of the dishes were very different.

Nandini worked on the design and promotion taking help from her mother's notes. She planned to have aboriginal art along with traditional Bengali style paintings. The restaurant was not only a gastronomic fusion but an artistic visual fusion too!

As the project took shape Nandini was happier, and her blood pressure remained under control. Robin's parents were quietly watching their son's dream take shape.

Everything was going fine until Robin's dad asked the most difficult question, "How are you planning to fund this project, Rob?"

Robin didn't have an answer to this question. The banks hadn't yet responded to his loan applications and he and Nandini didn't have much savings.

"Hmmm…don't really think we need big money." Robin answered.

To which Robin's dad said, "Well you do…have you worked out the budget yet? You have to buy all the cooking stuff, tables and chairs and rent space…the interior design work… And don't forget, marketing and promotion requires a fair amount of investment!"

Robin said, "I haven't done the final calculations but roughly we would need around two hundred thousand dollars to complete the project."

Robin's mother was watching TV. She casually said, "Why don't you help Rob with some money? He is working so hard."

"Two hundred thousand is a lot of money Sophiya. I don't have that kind of money.

He needs to take a loan. Let me check. I will get back to you Rob."

Robin knew his dad had worked very hard all his life and saved for his retirement. Moreover, Robin had little experience to take up such a big project. His dad probably didn't want to risk his savings with this project.

In the meantime, the loan from one of the banks was declined. Rob's dreams were falling apart. He was stressed but didn't share it with Nandini.

Robin looked very depressed. Nandini could see that on his face and his actions. She could guess the tension was all about money. She also found the Bank rejection letter in Robin's drawer. She decided to finally tell everything to her father.

Next day Nandini called up her father in Kolkata and told him everything about their project from her mother giving messages in her dreams, to their loan getting rejected. Nandini's father was moved by Nandini's love for her mother. He couldn't support his wife, but he made up his mind to support Nandini.

Nandini and her mother's dream became his dream too!

"Leave it with me…let me think over it. Let me see what I can do" Nandin's father said.

He couldn't sleep the whole night thinking about how he could help Nandini. He didn't have much money, but he had a share in his ancestral house. He thought of selling it and renting a one bedroom flat somewhere nearby.

Next morning, he called his brothers to his room and let them know his decision. His brothers were surprised.

His elder brother said "This house is our family's pride. How could you even think like that?"

"I have no option dada. My Nandini is sad. I have to support her and make her happy." said Nandini's dad.

"The value of the house is very high. None of us have that kind of money to buy you out and we don't want any outsider." The elder brother said.

The youngest brother jumped in "I think the best option is to sell the house as a whole and divide the money. There are plenty of developers who would be interested. Moreover, we have to move-on in life. This house is getting old, and we have to spend a lot of money, for maintaining this house. With the money, we receive, we can buy a new house or a flat. Life will be a lot easier!"

All the brothers agreed, even though they were sad to let go of the house that had been with their family for 150 years.

Next day after finishing his lunch, Nandini's dad was relaxing in his room. He was going through their old photo album. While looking at the photo of Nandini's mother, he was thinking about the good old days they had spent together. He heard a knock on the door. He looked up and saw Nandini's mother standing at the door. She looked very angry. She didn't say anything, just walked towards her dressing table, took the cupboard keys and opened her cupboard. She carefully took out a bank passbook and the locker keys and closed the cupboard back. She kept them on the table in front of Nandini's dad. She started walking away from him.

Nandini's father shouted, "Wait come back, don't leave me alone." She didn't stop. She walked out of the room, closing the door behind her.

There was a knock at the door Nandini's father woke up. The lady from the kitchen was standing at the door with a cup of tea. He realized that he had fallen asleep and whatever happened was a dream.

He sipped his tea thinking about the dream. Suddenly he remembered Nandini's mother took away the keys and a passbook. He quickly reached the dressing table to look for the keys. The keys were in place. Nandini's father felt relieved. He then opened the cupboard to see if there was any passbook. He found the Bank locker keys but no passbook. He took the keys in his hand "Was she trying to tell me something?" he wondered.

The Hidden Treasure

Next morning, Nandini's father visited the bank branch. The branch manager was glad to see him after a long time. Usually, the bank work was done by Nandini's mother. This was probably the first time Nandini's dad had come to the bank to operate the locker.

The bank manager welcomed him and offered his condolences, "Very sorry to hear about your loss sir."

"Well, it's all God's wish." replied Nandini's father. The Bank Manager then asked the helper to get two cups of tea. They talked about a few things and then they walked into the locker room. The bank manager helped him open the locker and walked out.

Nandini's father wasn't expecting much in the locker, probably some small pieces of jewellery that she got during her marriage and a few fixed deposit certificates. He opened the locker. There were three steel boxes nicely adjusted inside. Each box had jewellery carefully packed in cloth bags and documented. Inside those cloth bags there were necklace sets, bangles, and a variety of gold jewellery, which he had never seen before. He couldn't believe his eyes.

He knew Nandini's mother loved gold but how she collected so much of it was a mystery to him. He didn't recollect buying any big pieces of jewellery for Nandini's mother. He was shocked but at the same time he felt kind of euphoric because the gold mine that he found could help Nandini in fulfilling her mother's dream! But then before he could proceed any further, he had to find out how his wife got it! Where did she get all that money from?

He put everything back in the locker and locked it. He thanked the bank manager and came back home.

That night he called up Nandini and told her everything. Nandini was surprised.

"She probably accumulated all the gold for your marriage." Nandini's father said.

Nandini didn't answer. She asked, "*Baba*, are you sure you didn't find any bank passbook in ma's cupboard?"

"Nandu, there was no passbook in her cupboard!" He replied

"*Baba* then I suggest you ask the Bank manager if *ma* had any separate account with them. If she showed a passbook to you in the dream, there has to be a passbook somewhere." Nandini said.

Soul with a Mission

That evening Nandini's father searched the cupboard again and found a Bank passbook kept carefully under a stack of *sarees*. He took time to check it and he could solve the mystery very easily. He was proud of his wife and wished he had valued her talents when she was alive!

He immediately called Nandini. "You know Nandu what your mother did? She opened a separate account in which she put the money she got for writing in the magazine. I found her passbook under her stack of *sarees!* She started with a few hundred rupees but as her food column became popular, she earned a good amount of money. Every year she bought gold twice, before *Durga Puja* and during *nababarsho* (Bengali New Year). Her account has two nominees her husband and her daughter."

There was silence on both sides for some time. Nandini said, "I told you *baba, ma* is helping us in this project. She hasn't left us yet, whether anyone believes it or not."

Nandini's father said in a heavy voice, "hmm... I was thinking we were together for twenty-eight years, still she couldn't trust me for so many things. I was only her husband, could never become her friend...otherwise she wouldn't have kept so many secrets."

"No *baba*, she trusted you but not the society!" Nandini pacified her father.

"Anyways I will send you the money as soon as I can. Tell Robin. Hope you are taking care of yourself." Nandini's father ended the conversation.

Nandini's father did the final calculations adding up all his savings and the value of the jewellery. He found it was more than what was required. He didn't keep anything for himself because he got a monthly pension from the university.

He called for a meeting with his brothers and told them he had changed his plan. They were not selling the house. His eldest brother was very happy but the youngest one was a bit upset.

He said, "What made you change your plans overnight dada? And you seem to have solved your problem. Doesn't Nandu need the money anymore or have you found a goldmine?"

"Well, you can say I found a goldmine!" he answered. The brothers looked at each other. Nandini's father watched them but didn't say anything. He understood it would not be wise to tell them about the gold he has found, after all his wife kept everything a secret to stop people from talking!

He laughed and said, "I was joking… I have decided to send all the money I have, to Nandu. I will live on my pension."

"I don't think that will be right. What will happen if you fall sick? Medical treatments are very expensive." His younger brother said.

"You know for your *boudi* (sister-in-law), I spent only for the ambulance. She didn't even give time for one injection! We never know what's in store for us…life is so unpredictable." Nandini's father got emotional.

'And how are we going to manage the maintenance of this house?"

"We will continue to do it the way we did all these years. We will also have to ask the next generation to contribute. After all they are all well placed and are a part of this legacy! But for this year, I will pay for the repairing and colouring of the house because that was your *boudi's* last wish. She wanted to paint this house before Nandini's wedding in Kolkata!' Nandini's father put an end to the discussion.

Meanwhile in Melbourne it was yet another Sunday morning. Robin's dad casually asked him, "What happened with the project, Rob? No more fusion cooking? Have you finally put it on hold?"

"Not really…we are going a bit slow. Nandini's dad is giving us a good chunk of money. We are trying to arrange for the rest. I have put in a fresh application with one of the banks. Let's see."

"You asked money from Nandini's father? That's not a nice thing to do Rob." Robin's dad was upset.

"I never asked him, dad. He is giving on his own. And it's not his money, Nandini's mom left a big golden surprise for them!"

"Golden surprise! What does that mean?"

"That's a long story…" Robin was about to start.

"Wait Robin. I will tell Dad." Said Nandini and told them everything. For the first time she mentioned about the dreams and how her mother's soul guided them.

Robin's parents listened to Nandini with interest.

Robin's mother said, "Well, I don't believe much in all these, but since you are saying, it must be true. My child, I suggest that you don't think much about all this right now. Just keep calm for a few more days. It might affect your health."

Robin's dad said, "Yes and Nandini my dear, you can't be guided by a soul in something that involves such a lot of money! I understand your emotions but suppose, God forbid the restaurant does not run the way we are thinking, then what will happen? I believe success and failure will depend on how good you are. No one will help, but you!"

"I understand dad, what you are saying," Robin and Nandini kept their head down.

Robin's dad continued, "Your father is willing to invest because he is emotionally caught. Everything happened so suddenly he must be still in a state of shock, but Robin and you have to think more practically."

Nandini knew whatever Robin's parents said was correct, even she wouldn't have believed it, if it hadn't happened to her.

She kept quiet. She couldn't see her mother's dream come true in the near future.

Robin could understand Nandini's state of mind. He said, "Don't worry Nandini. I am sure something will happen. It is just a matter of time. We need to have more patience." Robin didn't want Nandini to get stressed.

Robin's dad smiled, "Well who wants to listen to my story now?"

"Yes please. I am waiting to hear that, not sure about others!" said Robin's mom while working in the kitchen. Suddenly the energy level in the room changed.

"Well, you know, we parents are very emotional about our children. I am sure your mother would agree with me. I have been trying to find the right moment to announce this."

Robin and Nandini exchanged glances.

Robin's dad continued," Well I checked and did my calculation. I will be able to spare 50K for your project."

Robin and Nandini were astounded. Robin almost jumped out of the chair. He hugged his father and said, "Thank you Dad. Thanks for trusting me. This money will be a loan on me. I shall return it as soon as possible."

"I am not in a hurry. You must return your father-in-law's money first, but before that you need to arrange the rest of the money."

"Yes, Dad I am quite hopeful that the bank will respond this time. Let's see. But thank you very much." Robin was grateful.

"Thank your mom, Rob. She actually blackmailed me to do this." Robin's dad said.

"I never blackmailed you Shubho! I just asked you a simple question. Who do you think you are saving all your money for? You said, who else but them. So, I said, then why not give them the money, when they need it? And you decided to give!" Rob's mom smiled.

"Mom you are a genius! Only you know the way to handle this rich old man." Robin laughed.

During the week Robin went for a meeting with the bank manager. He said that the chances of the loan getting sanction was bleak because Robin had no financial security. The case would be stronger if he found a partner who had a better financial status. Robin was quite demoralized. He was depending much on the loan!

He then talked to his parents and Nandini and told them what the bank manager said.

Rob's father said, "Finding a partner is a good idea, then investment and risks both get shared. Talk to your friends I am sure many of them have the dream of having their own restaurant. That's the trend nowadays – to be your own boss."

"I don't have any friend like that…' Robin said.

"I think it's better that we forget about the project for now. We tried every possible route…" Nandini was sad and disappointed.

There was an eerie silence in the room. Rob's dad didn't react further. Somewhere deep inside, he was relieved. He wasn't quite sure about the success of the project.

The next morning Robin's dad shared something which surprised everyone! He had a strange dream, the night before. He dreamt that he was getting the 'Young Entrepreneur' Award. The ceremony was taking place at the town hall. Everyone was congratulating him. He stood on the stage with Sophiya under the spotlight, as his citation was being read…

Robin's mother said, "So you had a lovely night mate!"

"Yes, it was lovely till I was asleep. Once I got up it started troubling me. It is true that I wanted to be an entrepreneur long back, when I was much younger. But now I am old! How can I become an entrepreneur now?"

"You still can become an entrepreneur Shubho," Robin's mother said on a serious note.

"Are you joking, Sophiya?' Robin's dad got irritated.

"Nope, my point is you can still become an entrepreneur if you become a partner in Rob's project."

"Are you serious? I don't have any more money!"

"Who is asking for money? Just become a partner in the Bank records and Rob will get the loan! We have our savings and this house. That's enough security for the bank loan!"

"Sophiya, I don't know what you are saying." Robin's father said

"I am saying, it is possible. I had already asked Robin to confirm from the bank and they have. You can become his partner!"

"Sometimes I wonder whether you ever realize that you are my wife too, and not just Rob's mother!"

"Yes of course, if you think of it, you will realize that by saying this I am trying to save my husband's money and put a liability on my son! If Robin gets the loan you will have to give much less than what you have decided to give…"

"Well, I am not promising anything till I talk to the bank, but the dream was too real! I can't just come out of it…"

"So, wasn't Robin there in the award ceremony?"

"I can't remember clearly but Nandini's mother was there for sure. She was among the spectators, smiling. It was so real." As he said this, he made everybody think about the belief, life after death.

Curious about the previous night's dream, Robin's father decided to talk to one of his close friends who was a retired professor of Physics. He had in the past conducted lots of research on transient energy and thermodynamics. He took special interest in the topic of the Afterlife and the behaviour of our soul as a form of pure energy.

His friend listened to the whole story and said, "Look, this universe and us, as humans, comprise two main components – matter and energy. We as human beings are a perfect amalgamation of both the forms. Our soul or *atma* is pure energy, whereas the body is matter. Our soul drives our body. Our emotions are governed by our soul whereas our actions and physical movements are looked after by our body. When we die, the connection between matter and energy is broken. The energy or soul is set free. I think in your case, the soul of Nandini's mother is not able to move on, after death. She probably has an unfinished business. But then this is not proven by science; it has come through experiences of people over a long period of time which ultimately became our faith!

Robin's dad was listening very carefully and asked, "But this is my first experience of this kind. This is so alien to me. Does it happen with everybody or are we special?"

His friend continued "Like you said when the lady was alive, she had to suppress a lot of her wishes because of her surroundings and relationships but after death she started expressing through dreams, because her soul became free. It didn't have to follow any rules and it is extremely powerful. I think she will move on once her work is done."

Full Speed Ahead

Robin's father agreed to become Robin's partner and applied for a joint loan which got sanctioned in no time. Everyone was happy. They decided to start the project immediately before the arrival of the new guest in the family.

Robin had already seen a few places for the restaurant. They chose the one close to the CBD. They had not yet chosen a name for it, but they wanted to include Nandini's mother's alias 'Sreelekha'.

One day Robin's father was recalling the whole episode and said, "Everything happened as if it were pre-planned. Nandini's mother had a dream to build her own restaurant, she got a chef son in law and then Nandini found her recipe book and things happened. It is all about getting connected…"

"Yes, I think you are right. In our case it's more about connecting through spices, Bengali recipes with native Australian spices…" Rob's mom added.

"I have found it," Nandini screamed with excitement. "We will name it '**The Spice Connect**' By Sreelekha and Rob"

Everyone loved the name. Robin quickly got the name registered. They didn't have much time. Nandini's pregnancy was in the eighth month. Robin was very busy with his restaurant and could spend little time with Nandini, but she didn't mind at all. She was on cloud nine because their dream project was taking shape. She spent most of the time with the little one inside her. She talked and sang and told stories to her baby the whole day and Robin joined them at night. Life had never been so beautiful!

It was autumn already and the leaves were changing colour. Flowers bloomed and there was an orange hue all around. *Durga Puja* was just a month away. They fixed the launch of the restaurant a day before *Durga Puja*.

The restaurant looked awesome with paintings and props portraying a mix of Indian and Aboriginal cultures. Robin and Nandini also decided a special menu for the launch day. Meanwhile Nandini's father arrived in Melbourne, and all waited for D-day!

Chapter 5

The Last Lap - Launch Day

On the launch day, Robin woke up very early in the morning. Nandini felt tired because she hadn't slept the whole night. She kept on thinking about her mother. It would have been so nice if her mother were alive to see the restaurant. She felt good that her mother would finally find peace.

Robin got ready but Nandini was feeling uneasy; her body was not under her control.

She rubbed her hand over her belly and whispered, "Today is our launch date, please don't come out today."

At this Robin smiled. He touched the baby and said, "Just one more day and Daddy will be all yours."

Nandini said, "Can I go a little later? I am feeling a little sluggish. You go with mom and dad. I will come with *baba* in a cab."

Robin thought for a while. He said, "No… I think I will let mummy also stay with you in case there is an emergency. The three of you can come together."

Robin and his dad reached the restaurant, the staff members were busy putting the finishing touches. Robin had invited about 100 guests for the inauguration including many senior members of the Bengali community in Melbourne.

The guests started coming. All of them loved the idea of fusion between the cultures.

Robin called Nandini to ask when they were coming. Nandini's father picked up the phone. He sounded nervous.

While on their way to the restaurant, Nandini felt some pain, so Robin's mom suggested that they visit the hospital once. The doctor checked Nandini and admitted her. Robin talked to his mom also. She asked Robin not to worry. Nandini was in labour, and the doctor said the baby would arrive not before late afternoon. So, Robin should do the launch nicely and reach the hospital on time.

Although his mother asked him not to worry, Robin was worried. He should have been with Nandini at this time, but he couldn't leave the launch party. It was very important for him. His dad welcomed the guests warmly, many of whom were his friends. Robin was there physically, but mentally he was with Nandini.

Robin's father was as anxious as him. He wanted to get the inauguration done with as soon as he possibly could. He too wanted to be with his daughter-in-law. He whispered to Robin to welcome everyone formally and give the inaugural speech. He picked up a glass and tapped with a spoon to attract everybody's attention.

Robin was on the stage that he had made for his inaugural speech. He held the microphone close to his mouth and took some time to start, "Welcome everybody to 'The Spice Connect.' I thank everyone for accepting my invitation today. The food that we will serve, is a collection of traditional Bengali dishes cooked in a mix of traditional Bengali and native Australian spices. We also have a few fusion dishes which are totally new and created by us, I hope you will like them." Everybody reacted with a big applause.

One of the Bengali ladies asked, "You know when I was in college, we used to get a women's magazine in which there was a column called 'Sreelekha's rannaghor' It was a very popular food column. In fact, I learnt most of my cooking from there. Is this restaurant related to that Sreelekha in any way?"

Robin answered after a pause "Yes, she is my mother-in-law. My wife would have loved to meet you, but she couldn't be here with us today. She is on a much bigger mission. We are going to have a baby and she is at the hospital now. My mom and her dad are with her. She is in labour as we inaugurate our restaurant here." Everybody responded with a big WOW and an applause followed.

Robin continued, "I hope you all enjoy this afternoon and don't forget to tell your friends and families about 'The Spice Connect'. Ours is the first restaurant that is experimenting with fusion cooking. Now, if you excuse me, I will leave you all here with my dad and friends. They will look after you. I will see you all later."

Somebody in the restaurant shouted, "Feel free to go Robin and be with Nandini. She needs you more."

Robin responded with a smile. He handed over the microphone to his dad, waved goodbye to all and walked out of the restaurant.

His dad continued, "At first, I hesitated to participate in this project but, a few things that have happened, has opened my eyes. Standing here I am proud today. Proud because we are launching two of my projects, that is very close to my heart. One, of course is this restaurant and Nandini is working very hard to deliver the second project successfully. I will be a proud grandfather very soon. I would request you all to wish us all the very best."

Robin couldn't wait to be with Nandini. As he sat in the car, he couldn't help but notice a green parrot sitting on a tree branch just outside their restaurant. As he turned on the car ignition and was about to start, he remembered Tiya in Nandini's house in Kolkata and her welcome call. He stopped and looked outside again; it was gone.

He drove through the busy streets and reached the hospital. Every minute seemed like an hour! He reached the fourth floor and as he came out of the lift, he heard a baby cry. He stopped. One of the nurses standing there asked "Are you the daddy?" Before Robin could answer his mom came out of the room. She gave Robin a hug.

"You've got a baby daughter, Rob. She is beautiful." Robin had tears in his eyes. His mother held his hand and pulled him inside the room.

Nandini was still in the delivery bed. The doctor had the little baby in his hand. He turned towards Robin and said "Perfect timing dad. Please come here, you have to now cut the umbilical cord. The nurse handed the scissors over to Robin. He was a bit nervous, but he held up straight and strong. He cut the cord. The doctor then handed over the baby to the nurse.

Robin then kissed Nandini. "Congratulations mummy" and Nandini replied, "Congratulations daddy." Robin gave her a big hug.

Robin held Nandini's hand and asked, "How do you feel?" She smiled, "I feel like a truck just ran over me. But it's all worth it."

Robin left Nandini and the baby with the nurse and came out. His mom and Nandini's father were waiting there. Nandini's father looked happy, but his eyes were teary. He was probably missing his wife. Robin sat beside him, thinking what to say to comfort him.

After a while Nandini and the baby were shifted to a room. Nandini looked relaxed and happy. Robin's mother got busy with the little one. Nandini asked her father," Did you call Kolkata?"

Nandini's father remembered he hadn't given the good news to the rest of the family yet! Robin dialled Nandini's uncle's number and gave the phone to him.

Nandini's father proudly announced, "Hello, can you hear me? I have become a grandfather. Nandini and her baby girl are both doing fine. It looks like your *boudi* (sister-in-law) has come back as her daughter! Remember what she said after her Australia visit? What a beautiful country! In my next birth I want to be born there!" After a brief pause, he continued "That's the reason she left in such a hurry leaving me all alone." He cried like a child.

Seeing Nandini's father visibly upset, Robin took the phone from him and talked to Nandini's uncle. He asked if everything was good out there.

Nandini's uncle said, "All good but there is one bad news! Tiya is gone. This morning when we woke up, the cage door was open, and she was not there!"

Robin had goosebumps all over. He remembered seeing a parrot outside the restaurant. 'Tiya and Nandini's mother indeed had a soul connection', he thought.

By then Robin's dad had reached the hospital. He was overjoyed to see his little princess. He made a lot of noise and said, "Oh my god she is so beautiful! Sophiya…now you will see what I mean when I say, 'Bengali beauty'…just let her grow up!"

Everybody broke into laughter. Just then the nurse entered, and everybody became quiet. She said, "Excuse me all, I didn't mean to disturb you… I got a question for mum and dad? I was wondering what name I shall put for the birth certificate?"

Robin and Nandini looked at each other. They were so busy with the restaurant they hadn't thought of any name for their baby! There was a big silence in the room.

Robin's dad watched them and said, "Sister in our family, the grand dad will choose the name not mum and dad! My little princess will be called 'Sreelekha – Sreelekha Bannerjee'. Give me the form I will write it."

Nandini and her father were overwhelmed. There couldn't be a better way to pay tribute to Nandini's mother!

And the story continues...

'The Spice Connect' completed two years and so did Robin and Nandini's little princess, Sreelekha! The restaurant has been doing very well and was quite popular.

By the way, it won the 'Restaurant of the year' award during the second year and Robin's father got to go up on the stage to receive the award with his son and daughter-in-law!

Nandini had left her job and started helping Robin full time, at the restaurant. She picked up new skills helping customers and managing the counter. All the mathematics that she learnt in her school, was helping her now.

One busy morning she received a call from a Mahender Singh. He wanted 'The Spice Connect' to cater for his granddaughter's twenty first birthday celebrations. He wanted a good spread of fusion dishes for fifty people for the occasion.

Spice Connect had never done catering before. Nandini was hesitant and couldn't make up her mind.

"Well, I have been to your restaurant a couple of times, and I like the food." He said.

"But Sir, we haven't done any catering yet, so I am not sure…"

Before Nandini could complete her sentence, he said, "There is always a first time for everything my dear."

Nandini decided to take the order.

The Golden Key

Chapter 1

Yamini's 21ˢᵗ Birthday

There was festivity at the Jones family residence in Melbourne. Yamini Jones, the elder daughter of Michael and Chanda, was turning twenty-one! The house was full of guests. Yamini's uncles, aunties and cousins and a couple of her close friends, were already there.

Yamini had completed her Pharmacy degree a year ago and was working as an assistant in a drug manufacturing company. She was a smart, independent and practical girl. She felt a bit uncomfortable celebrating her 21ˢᵗ birthday so grandly. According to her, 18 was the age of majority (becoming an adult) and she had already celebrated that with grandiosity! She thought this was just a waste of money.

Yamini or Mini as she was called by all, was the eldest among all the children in her generation, so this was the first celebration of its kind. Everyone was very excited about it, especially the younger lot. They were busy deciding on the dresses they were going to wear that evening. They also tried to advise Mini, but she didn't pay heed.

Yamini's brother Sam, who was four years younger to her, was most excited. He was gathering tips for his eighteenth birthday party which was going to happen the year after. Not only the young, but the elders were also busy. They were busy preparing their little speeches to be delivered after the 'handing over of the key' function.

The "Handing over of Key" function signified freedom. The person who celebrated the 21st birthday, was now entitled to come in and go out of the house as he or she pleased.

Mini enjoyed watching all her cousins in action but was waiting eagerly for one person – her *Nanaji* (maternal grandfather), Mr. Mahender Singh. She loved him very dearly and considered him a role model.

Mini heard a car on the driveway. She looked out of the window and ran to the door. Nanaji's white Mercedes Benz E240, 2005 model stopped in the driveway and out came an old man gracefully dressed in a dark coloured suit and a golf hat. He had gun-metal grey hair and bright gleaming eyes. As Mini received him, he kissed her forehead and congratulated her on turning twenty-one. Mini was his most favourite for the simple reason that she was his eldest grandchild.

By then everyone, young and old, had come out to welcome him. Mini held her Nanaji's hands and walked with him to the living room. Mahender Singh settled down on his favourite sofa. He was very happy to see all the relatives of both families, Singhs and Jones together. He asked about everyone's well-being.

"*Ma* nanaji is here" Mini shouted. Her mother was in the kitchen organising food for the crowd. She answered back, "Yes, I know. Give me 5 mins."

As nanaji relaxed after his long drive, his elder daughter Chanda (Mini's mother) entered with a cup of tea for her dad, in his favourite silver crockery. Her sister Tara, Mahender

Singh's second daughter, followed her with a tray of cookies. Everyone took their tea and sat around him.

Whenever there was a family gathering, it kind of became a ritual and an unwritten protocol that everybody would leave all work and have their tea with Nanaji. He would invariably share his stories which were full of life lessons. He had the most incredible journey of life, through seven decades! He had seen numerous ups and downs in his life but never lost his big and bright smile!

Everyone sipped their tea and were waiting for Nanaji to start a story. Suddenly Mini asked, "Nanaji, did you also celebrate your 21st birthday?"

Mahender Singh smiled and shook his head. "No. In our times, celebrating birthdays was not so common among most families! Only the Royals and the rich celebrated their birthdays with pomp and show. Ours was more of a small family affair. I remember, on my birthdays, my mother would pray to God for my wellbeing and cook my favourite *Kheer* (pudding with rice, milk, and sugar). She would also put nuts and raisins to make it special. I would then touch the elders' feet and seek their blessings. And yes…on my birthdays I wasn't asked to study, I could play as much as I wanted, and we got lots of food to eat!"

"Nanaji tell us what you did on your 21st birthday?" Sam asked.

Nanaji smiled again, "Nothing much Sam… I remember on my 21st birthday I had gone for a job interview. I did quite well in the interview but couldn't get that job. I came back home, depressed. My mother had made my favourite rice pudding, like every year. That year for the first time I prayed to God. I prayed for a decent job because I knew I couldn't get one without his help. Those days there were not many jobs in the market and there were thousands of contenders for just one position!"

"You are lucky Mini, you already have a job and are going to get the keys of the house too!" Sam felt jealous and teased Mini.

"That's only a tradition Sam. I already have the keys and can come and go as I please." Mini answered.

"You are right Mini, but remember traditions reinforce our value system. The key that you are going to get this evening is not just the house key, but it is the key to an adult life and the independence that comes with it. Remember by handing over the key to you the family also expects you to take responsibility." Nanaji explained.

Mini agreed with her nanaji. She waited for the celebrations.

The Celebrations

Mini's parents, Michael and Chanda had arranged everything to make their daughter's 21st birthday celebrations special. The party was expected to go on the whole night and would finish after lunch the next afternoon. The elders could get some sleep if they wished but the younger generation decided to party the whole night.

The main living room was decorated tastefully with flowers and ribbons. A wishing tree in silver and gold was kept in one corner for everyone to write messages. A collage of Mini's photographs adorned one of the walls. The chocolate cake looked stunning. It was decorated with a set of golden keys. The food chosen were all Mini's favourite dishes.

Yamini was in her room, getting ready for the evening. The party was about to start. Everyone waited for her customary arrival! As the clock struck six and started chiming, Yamini entered. She looked like a princess in a beautiful light blue dress.

Chanda couldn't take her eyes off Yamini! She couldn't imagine her little Mini was now 21! Everyone clapped and welcomed her.

Mini stood in the middle of the room facing her parents and everybody else gathered around them. It was time for handing over the keys of the house! Michael and Chanda were ready with two boxes which had the keys! Michael said, "You'll always be my superstar love. Whatever you do in life, I'm sure you'll go far. Congratulations on reaching one of life's biggest milestones! Happy 21st birthday!"

Chanda got emotional. With teary eyes she said, "No matter how many birthdays come and go, you'll always be my little girl. Have a wonderful birthday. May God bless you with all that you wish for! I love you very much!"

Michael took out the keys from the box and handed them over to Mini. She hugged her father, and he kissed her forehead.

Chanda now gave her the second box too. "Another one, wow two sets of keys?" she said. She opened it and found a key pendant in gold!

"Wow this is beautiful. Now I need a gold chain." She said and hugged her mother as tears rolled down her cheeks.

Everyone clapped and sang the 21st birthday song:

> 21 today, 21 today,
> She's got the key of the door,
> Never been 21 before.

Father says, she can do as she likes
So hip hip hooray
She's the queen of the castle
21 today!

All the relatives and friends gave gifts to Mini. Some gave speeches, some said poems, while a few sang for her.

Nanaji was watching everyone, all the while and enjoying. Once everybody had wished, he came close to Mini. He said, "May the key 21 help you to 'unlock' your future and become the key to happiness. I hope that the path ahead is bright and kind. May the gold key pendant remind you *the golden rules of life* always! Happy birthday sweetheart!"

Mini hugged her grandfather. "I didn't know what gift to give you, so I booked a lunch from 'The Spice Connect' for all of us. They will deliver the food around 12 tomorrow." Nanaji said. Everyone shouted with joy. Sam said, "Mini, you have a double celebration!"

Yamini thanked Nanaji and everyone else for their lovely gifts and all that they did to make her birthday such a memorable one! "Okay everybody, it's now time to cut the cake," said Chanda. Michael had ordered a double tiered cake. Yamini blew out the candle and cut the cake.

A champagne bottle was opened for the occasion. Mini poured champagne in two flutes. She held one in each hand and walked up to nanaji. "One for you nanaji. Cheers!" She said and sat next to him sipping champagne. She asked, "What golden rules were you talking about nanaji?"

"What do you mean?" nanaji asked.

"Remember, the golden rules that you referred to during the key ceremony. Oh nanaji, you are getting old."

"Oh ok, that one."

"Leave it nanaji, I will google it."

Nanaji said smiling, "You won't find the golden rules on the internet. They are the golden rules that I have learnt in my life. My keys to a happy and successful life."

"Ok, then you tell me now" Mini said. Mini's brother and cousins could sense that there was some interesting conversation going on between nanaji and Mini. They all came and sat around them, hoping to hear some interesting stories.

Mahender Singh thought for a while and said, "According to me the key to happiness lies in our hands. The four rules or keys of happiness are Love, Learning or Knowledge, Honesty and Hope. Follow these four rules and you will always be happy and keep the family together."

Everyone was quiet. They were trying to think what it meant! "Which one do you think is the most important one?" asked nanaji.

The room went quiet again waiting for him to continue. "The most important is hope. Without hope everything falls apart."

The silence was broken by one of Yamini's cousins, "nanaji, can you throw some more light on it?"

"Yes! I will give you an example. You study well with a hope that you will pass in the examination and get a good job after you finish studies. Right?"

"Yes." Everyone answered in chorus.

"So, if the hope wasn't there, you wouldn't study." Mahender smiled. Everybody nodded in agreement. "I am sure everybody understands what Love is. It keeps a family together in good times and bad." Everybody nodded.

"Honesty is something that you practice at home and at your workplace. Without honesty there is no trust or credibility. Honesty also reflects your education and the values that you are brought up with and, you in turn, impart to your children."

It was getting very late. Everybody was tired and sleepy. Nanaji promised them that he would tell them stories to explain each point in detail the next day.

That night Mahender Singh couldn't sleep. Mini's key had unlocked the door of his memories. His theory was born out of his own life experiences. All his stories were real!

Chapter 2

Love

It was in the early seventies when Mahender Singh finished his degree, and he was desperately looking for a job. His father was going to retire within a year. He lived with his parents and a younger sister. His sister was studying in the local college. His commerce degree and good character certificates from his school and college that said that he was an intelligent, hardworking and honest person could not get him any decent job.

He had been a very good hockey player in school and college. He had also represented Delhi in a few national level tournaments. He would have loved to become a full-time hockey player, but he couldn't afford to. His father was a petty clerk in a company and didn't have enough savings. Being the only son in the family, Mahender had to take charge. Moreover, those days sport was not considered a serious career option. His father always said '*Paroge likhoge banoge nawab, kheloge kudoge banoge kharab*' (If you read and write you will live like a king, if you play you will ruin your life!)

Mahender decided to change his strategy. To promote sports, every bank had a few positions for candidates with strong sports background. He decided to apply for jobs under the '*sports quota*'. He started his hockey practice once again. It was a wise decision. Soon he passed the Probationary Officer examination in one of the large Public Sector Banks and was selected. He proved the old saying wrong and thanked his stars that he never stopped playing. He was also happy that he could now continue his passion along with his job.

Mahender was a hard-working young man, who was willing to learn. Soon he became a favourite of his seniors. Also, his helping attitude and sense of humour made him popular among his co-workers. His passion for work soon became his religion.

He followed a strict daily routine. He woke up every morning at 5 and went for his morning exercises and hockey practice sessions at the local club. After finishing his morning routine, he would have a shower and be ready at the breakfast table, sharp at 7.30 am. His mother would cook the healthiest breakfast for him and pack some food for his lunch.

He would reach his office well before his manager came. He would never leave any files pending. He was learning all the tricks to be a good banker. His life as a sports person helped him a lot. To be successful in both banking and sport, one needed to be disciplined and humble and had to follow the rules of the book and Mahender had those qualities.

Mahender was doing well at work and his parents were very happy. His mother started looking for a girl for him so that he could settle down and have a family. She wanted to see little grandchildren running around in the house soon.

As soon as the relatives and neighbours came to know that Mahender's mother was looking for a girl for him, proposals started pouring in. Mahender's parents went and met a few of them but none of them materialised. According to them, Mahender needed a gentle traditional girl who would take care of Mahender and the family.

Mahender on the other hand, wanted a wife who was educated and modern, preferably working and had a mind of her own. Mahender after a lot of hesitation told his mother about his preference.

Search for a Wife

One morning while serving breakfast Mahender's mother said, "*aj jaldi aa sakte ho kaam se? Ladki dekhne jana hai.* (Can you come a bit early from work today? We have to go to see a girl today.)"

"*Aap aur papa kyo nahi dekh lete pehle? Agar apko pasand aye fir mai jaunga. Kam me problem hota hai.* (Why don't papa and you go first? If you both like I will go. Why disturb me and my work?)" Mahender didn't show much interest.

"*Agar tuney apne liye ladki dekh lee hoti to kitna achch hota. Tere demand bhi to koi kam nahi. Tere sarey dosto ki shadi ho gayee hai.* (If you had found a girl for yourself, our life would be lot easier. Your demands are also no less. Most of your friends are already married.)" His mother got a bit irritated.

Mahender listened to his mother and agreed. He could understand that his mother was looking for a girl of his choice. He asked casually, "*Kya karti hai?* (What does she do?)"

"*School me teacher hai.* (She is a teacher in a school.)"

"*Hmm. Kitne baje jana hai?* (Hmm. What time do we have to go?)"

"*Sham 5 baje.* (Around 5 in the afternoon!)"

"*Acha pahunch jaunga!* (Ok I will be there.)

Mahender picked up his lunch box, put on his helmet, started his bike and left for work. As promised, he was back home on time.

Mahender wore his best pair of trousers and shirt and rubbed some aftershave and called for a black and yellow taxi. His father sat up front while he sat with his mother in the rear seat.

While in the taxi, Mahender asked his father "*Papa apke pass ladki ki biodata hai?* (Papa, have you got a biodata of the girl?)" His father handed him a paper. "*Ye ladki ki biodata. Maine dekh liya hai. Achi family hai. Agar wo log puchey, isliye dekh lo* (This is the girl's biodata. I have checked it. The family is very good. In case they ask just go through it once)" His father said.

Mahender took the piece of paper but hesitated to look at it. His mother said, "*Arey pehle kyo nahi diya. Shadi usne karni hai humne nahi. Beta padh le dhyan se aur bata kaisi lagi* (Why didn't you give it to him earlier? After all he is going to get married to her, not us! Mahender read it carefully and tell me if you like it.)"

The girl's name was Suniti. She was a primary teacher in a neighbourhood English medium school and her hobbies were cooking, sewing and gardening. She was the youngest among four children. She had three elder brothers, out of whom two were married. Her father had a family business and they lived in a joint family in the Old Delhi area.

Mahender read all of it, in one go. He wasn't impressed. The biodata was not up to his expectation. He was hoping that she had more sophisticated hobbies like reading and listening to music, but he didn't say anything. His mother was looking at his face for his reaction. Mahender smiled at his mother. She became happy and the grin on her face got wider.

Mahender thought, "She teaches in an English medium school…so I am sure she can speak in English, if not fluent." He was kind of happy, because none of his friends' wives could speak English and didn't work. His mother could sense that he was thinking something. She advised him "*Kuch puchna ho to puch lena. Achey log hai. Bura nahi manenge.* (Ask the girl whatever you want to ask. They are good people. They won't mind.)"

Mahender agreed with a nod.

The taxi took them through the narrow and busy 'Old Delhi' Streets. It stopped in front of a *Haveli* (large old house / traditional Indian mansion). As they got off, it felt like the whole neighbourhood was waiting for them. All the neighbours were on the rooftops or in the street, getting a glimpse of the potential groom for Suniti. Mahender was very conscious. As they walked through the open courtyard, Mahender felt like a superstar, only the red carpet was missing. After the courtyard, they had to walk through a long veranda and then they reached a large living room.

As they walked in, they were greeted by the girl's parents, Mr. and Mrs. Sharma.

Mahender's father said "Your house reminds me of our ancestral house. *Ludhiana me hamara bilkul aisa hi ghar hai* (We have a similar house in Ludhiana.)"

Mr. Sharma smiled. "Our family has been living in this house for four generations." he said.

Mahender's father looked up at the ceiling. He was impressed, "You have maintained the house very well. So, you have a joint family here?" he asked.

Mr. Sharma replied "*Parents nahi rahe. Hum char bhai hai.* (My parents are no more. We are four brothers.) Three of us live here supporting our family business. My youngest brother lives in Bangalore. We have a chain of sweet shops in Delhi. We have been making Indian sweets for many generations. Our sweet shop here is more than a hundred years old." said Suniti's father proudly.

Mahender was amused. "*Halwai ke ghar me teacher* (A teacher in a family of confectioners.) What an odd combination!!"

There were 4 doors in the room. Mahender knew that his bride-to-be was going to walk through one of those doors, he just didn't know which one. Mahender looked around keeping a close watch on those doors, one at a time. He just couldn't wait to meet the girl.

The walls were adorned with some old photographs and water colours. Just above one of the doors, on the wall, was a big painting of Goddess *Laxmi* (Goddess of wealth). She was kind of smiling on Mahender. He loved the smile and he felt Goddess Lakshmi was blessing him from up there. As he looked down, he saw Suniti walk in through that door. She had a tray full of sweets. Following her, was their maid with cups of tea on a tray.

Suniti had covered her head and half her face, with her *dupatta* (cloth covering a woman's head). Mahender tried hard to get a glimpse of her face. All he could see was her pink lips, which had a light smile on it. Mahender wanted to look a little longer, but he decided to take his eyes off. He was sure Suniti could see him through her dupatta although he couldn't see her face. "Why is the world so unfair with boys?" He thought.

Suniti offered sweets to everybody sitting there, including Mahender. Then she touched her elders' feet and got their blessings. A chair was already kept for her next to Mahender's seat. Suniti sat on the chair. She was a bit uneasy.

Mahender was frozen, he could neither talk, nor turn his head. Everybody else talked freely. Right in front of him, at a distance, was a glass cabinet where he could see Suniti's reflection. He did gather some courage a couple of times and he looked up to see her reflection. But he realised that people might think badly about him.

Suniti's mother said, "*Suniti bahot intelligent ladki hai. Topper thi apni school aur college me.* (Suniti is a very intelligent girl. She has always been a topper in her school and college.) She wanted to do her MBA degree. But you know in our family, women are not allowed to work. After a lot of discussion, her father allowed Suniti to become a teacher and work in our neighbourhood school."

Mahender was quiet and absorbing everything that was said about Suniti.

Mahender's father said, "*Hum log kaafi dino se dekh rahey hai. Ajkal bachcho ke demand bahot badh gaye* (We are searching for a girl for some time now. Nowadays kids have big demand.) In our times, we just married the first girl we saw." Everybody laughed.

Suniti's dad nodded in agreement and said, "We also had a couple of marriage proposals for her, but Suniti was adamant about one thing, she wanted to marry a professional and not a businessman. So, when my sister said that your son worked in the bank, we were very keen!"

Mahender's mother smiled. "Even we were interested because my son wanted a working girl…"

Mahender interrupted his mother. "*Ma* I never said I wanted a working girl. I just wanted somebody who was educated and…" He didn't want Suniti to think bad about him.

"Does that mean that you don't want your wife to work?" Suniti asked.

"No…it is not that…" Mahender didn't know what to answer. He decided to keep quiet.

"If you want to ask any question, feel free my son," Mr. Sharma told Mahender.

"No Sir, I don't have anything to ask," replied Mahender.

The parents then talked among themselves on different topics and Mahender and Suniti listened to them. After a couple of hours of talking and good food, it was time to head back home. Suniti's father asked one of the boys to go and get a taxi. As they walked out of the main door, Mahender and Suniti walked side by side. One of Suniti's aunts said, "This is a match made in heaven. They look great as a couple." Everybody kind of agreed.

While coming back home in the taxi Mahender was quiet. His father looked happy and so was his mother. She was repeating everything that Suniti's mother had said about her. "*Ab tu chup kyo hai, Mahender?* (Why are you so quiet Mahender?)" She asked.

Mahender's father knew exactly what the problem was. He had been through it all! He took out an envelope from his pocket and gave it to him.

"What is it?" Mahender asked

"*Khol ke dekh lo* (Just open it and see)" His father said.

Mahender looked at Suniti's photograph. She was pretty with expressive eyes and a beautiful smile. Mahender looked at his mother and smiled. His face lit up.

"*Pasand ayee?* (Did you like her?)" She asked. Mahender nodded to say, 'Yes'.

The parents agreed to proceed with the wedding. To make it formal, Mahender's father visited Suniti's house for the *"Roka ceremony"* (a ceremony where the boy, the girl and both their families formally agree to go ahead with the marriage). The families exchanged gifts. That was the beginning of the relationship.

With folded hands Suniti's father asked Mahender's father if he had any particular wish, he would be happy to fulfill.

Mahender's father answered with pride, "With God's grace we have everything. My son earns enough to buy whatever we wish for. We just wish for a girl who will make a good wife to him and a daughter to us."

Wedding Celebrations

It was a major event in the house, Mahender was getting married. Everyone was very excited. Mahender's father wanted to spend from his savings, but Mahender didn't agree. He took a loan from the bank. He knew Suniti's parents were rich and they would spend lavishly for their only daughter's marriage. Mahender didn't want his parents to feel lesser in any way. He also wanted to buy decent gifts for everyone – his parents, his younger sister and of course Suniti.

Though he took a loan Mahender was a bit tense about what Suniti' family was planning. They shouldn't spend extravagantly, he thought. Being a banker, he always thought of finance before doing anything.

He quietly visited her school one day to talk to her about how she was and how were all the arrangements going.

Suniti was shocked to see Mahender waiting outside the school gate. She didn't want her colleagues and students to see her talking to a young man. She walked past him in a hurry and whispered, "Follow me." Mahender followed her quietly till she stopped round a corner and said, "I am sorry I won't be able to go out with you, my family will not like it. It's a matter of a few more days…" Mahender was embarrassed.

He quickly asked for forgiveness and said, "My purpose in coming here is completely different. I just wanted to let you know that we are okay with a decent traditional marriage. Let your father not spend unnecessarily." Suniti listened to Mahender and walked away with that gentle smile on her face. Mahender couldn't but appreciate her presence of mind.

As the Marriage Day got closer, Mahender became busier and the activities around the house increased. Their house was very old. All the cracks in the walls and the weathered nooks and corners were fixed. The house also got a fresh coat of paint. Mahender was assigned a separate bedroom. It was decorated with flowery curtains and new furniture.

The relatives started arriving in the house, a week before the date. Mahender had hired a guest house nearby, to accommodate the extra guests. A big *langar* (community kitchen) was set up in the courtyard. There was a festive atmosphere. The whole street was celebrating Mahender's wedding.

Mahender had invited all his work colleagues and his hockey team mates for his wedding. His manager at work was very happy for him. He also indicated a salary increase after his marriage. He knew that expenses would go up after marriage. Mahender was very grateful.

Suniti's family had booked a wedding hall near their house for the marriage. The venue was decorated with flowers and colourful lights. His friends from the hockey club had sponsored the photography for the event. Mahender's dad wanted the wedding to be a gala event. He was his only son.

On the wedding day, Mahender started his journey from his house in a car, decorated with flowers. About a kilometre before the wedding venue, Mahender got out of car and rode on a white mare. The wedding Band moved on foot, playing Bollywood songs, in front of Mahender. All of Mahender's friends and relatives danced to the beats of the band.

At the entrance to the wedding venue Mahender's family was welcomed with floral garlands and sprinkling of rosewater. Mahender was then escorted by Suniti's brothers to a stage and made to sit on a big chair quite like a throne. He was the king of the night. One by one, all of Suniti's family members came and greeted Mahender. Just next to him there was another seat which was vacant, meant for Suniti, the Queen of the night. Suniti joined him after about half an hour. Her coming was made grand by her friends walking with her. Her brothers led the way holding a decorated cloth over her head. She was looking gorgeous in a red silk *lehnga* (Indian dress).

On reaching the stage Mahender and Suniti exchanged floral garlands. They were the centre of all attention. Their friends and relatives wished them and gave them gifts. There were food and drinks in plenty. Everyone enjoyed and most left around midnight.

Then started the wedding rituals. It started with *Kanyadan,* a ceremony during which the father of the bride gives her to her groom. Suniti's father placed her hands into Mahender's hands as a gesture of giving her away. Mahender could see Suniti and her father becoming emotional. He held her hand firmly to tell her that he would always be there with her.

The priest performed many other rituals around a *havan* (religious fire lit for prayers), chanting mantras. By the time all the rituals got over, it was early morning. It was time for "Vidai" – time for Suniti to say goodbye to her family and move to her husband's house. Everybody in the family was sad, so was Suniti.

Suniti took handfuls of rice and coins and threw them over her head to show her appreciation for the time and love given to her in the home of her parents. She was now ready to start a new life with her husband. Suniti's family gave her a tearful farewell.

It was early morning when Suniti reached Mahender's house. She was welcomed warmly by Mahender's parents, his sister and their relatives. Suniti was a bit worried and nervous. She was unsure of all the new responsibilities, but Mahender's mother and sister made her feel at home.

Honeymoon

Mahender's office friends had organised a romantic 3-day honeymoon for the newly wedded couple in Shimla (It is the capital city of the North Indian state of Himachal Pradesh, situated at a height of 2276 m. It was declared as the Summer Capital of British India. This hilly town is a premier honeymoon destination for newly married couples).

Mahender and Suniti started their honeymoon with a rickshaw ride from their house to the station. Then, they boarded a train to Kalka (the terminus station for Delhi-Kalka train line, situated at a height of 658 m.) and hired a car from Kalka to reach Shimla. The journey was long and tiring but both of them enjoyed it.

The hotel was situated on a hillside. They now had to climb steep stairs, about 20 meters. Mahender held Suniti's hand firmly and their big heavy bag was on his shoulder. He was learning to take on the responsibilities to support his new family.

They checked into a beautiful hotel that had big rooms with high ceiling, reminiscent of the colonial architecture. It used to be an old government guest house before India's independence. All the big *babus* (bureaucrats) and British Indian officers spent their summer days in that guest house. The room had a few doors. Mahender thought of exploring them, but Suniti was very tired, she wanted to relax. Mahender agreed and sat next to Suniti as she watched television. They had their dinner and went to bed thereafter. Mahender was a bit hesitant and uncomfortable. So was Suniti. They were alone. This was the first time they were sharing a bed.

The next morning Mahender got up. He was expecting to see Suniti next to him, but she wasn't in bed. One of the doors in the room was open. It was a chilly morning. The sun was rising, and sunlight fell on the floor through the open door. He could hear the birds chirping.

Wondering what happened he walked up to the door and out of the room. There was a garden right outside that door. As he walked out, he saw Suniti standing at the end of the garden, staring at the rising sun. The view was marvellous.

The big orange sun was bright and glowing as if highlighting the beginning of their new life together. He took a big deep breadth and said, "Oh there you are!"

Suniti turned around and said, "Come… I have never seen such a colourful sun!"

Mahender joined her. Suniti gently held his hand, and both watched the sun rise together. Time just froze for them.

After a few seconds, Suniti shouted to one of the helpers in the hotel, *"Bhaiya chai leke aao!* (Brother, get some tea)!"

"Ji Abhi laya (Ok getting it)" he replied.

Mahender and Suniti talked, as they sipped their tea. That was like the perfect beginning of the day and their life together.

The next two days in Shimla just flew. They visited all the tourist places and romantic lookouts around Shimla. Suniti wanted to thank the "All Mighty" for bringing them together. They visited all the temples in the area and offered their prayers. Mahender wasn't very religious, but he was learning to listen to and fulfil Suniti's wishes.

It was the third day of their honeymoon, and it was time to get back to reality. They returned home and slowly, got back to their daily routine. Mahender got busy with his bank and his hockey club. Suniti left her previous school and started looking for work in a school in her new neighbourhood.

Suniti now shared the household work with her mother-in-law. The breakfast was prepared by Mahender's mother, and Suniti cooked lunch and dinner for the whole family. Her sister-in-law was busy with her studies but every now and then she would help in cleaning the house and other household chores.

One evening Mahender came back from office to find Suniti sick and unwell. Mahender was worried till his mother told him that he was going to be a father. He was the happiest man. He ran to the nearby sweet shop and bought sweets for everybody in the house and gave some to his neighbours. They had a reason to celebrate again.

Suniti asked him whether he wanted a boy or a girl. "A boy of course! I will train him to be a hockey player like Dhyan Chand (famous Indian hockey player). I couldn't fulfil my dream… I will do it through my son!" He said with confidence. Suniti didn't say anything, she prayed to God to fulfil her husband's dream.

The Family Grew

It was a Monday. Mahender left for work as usual. Suniti was almost on the last lap of her pregnancy. She was helping her mother-in-law in the kitchen when she felt uneasy.

Mahender's mother knew it was time to take her to the hospital. She called up Mahender, but he was busy in a very important meeting. Mahender's parents and sister took her to the hospital. The doctor admitted her and put her on observation. The baby was on its way out. Mahender's sister tried calling him, but he seemed very busy. She also called Suniti's parents and asked them to come to the hospital.

Around evening, Suniti gave birth to a healthy and beautiful baby girl. Mahender got the news while in office. His sister had called and left the message with his assistant.

His assistant interrupted him while in his meeting, she said, "Congratulations! You have got a baby girl. Goddess Lakshmi has come to your house."

Mahender was unhappy, he wanted a boy, but then soon realised there was nothing he could do. He was learning to accept things as they came. He rode his scooter as fast as he could and reached the hospital.

His parents and Suniti's parents were sitting outside the room. As he arrived at the hospital everybody stood up and greeted him. He walked inside the room. Suniti was sleeping, tired from the gruelling experience. He looked around for the baby. The nurse entered the room with the baby, she had taken her for a quick bath.

The nurse gave the little girl to Mahender and said, "Your daddy has been running away from his responsibilities the whole day. Now he is going to take care of you." Mahender was embarrassed but smiled gently. He looked at his little girl. She was as beautiful as a Goddess. Mahender was in love at the very first sight. His emotions changed from being sad to a proud and happy father. He held her close to his chest, kissed her as tears rolled down his cheeks.

Mahender sat there with the baby on his lap. After some time Suniti woke up. "Oh, *Kab aye*? (When did you come?)" She asked.

Mahender said, "*Thodi der pehle*. (a little while ago.) Thank you very much for this precious gift. I am very happy!"

Suniti smiled but looked worried. She asked, "You wanted a boy. What will happen to your dream? Your Dhyan Chand?"

"Nothing I will redesign my dream! We will have a female hockey player named Chanda! I can't name her Dhyan so, what do you think of Chand with an 'a', *Chanda* (the moon)?"

Suniti responded with a big smile. Just as daddy stopped talking, little Chanda started crying. "Maybe she didn't like her name" Mahender said while handing over Chanda to Suniti. "No, don't worry, I think she is hungry," said Suniti. Chanda became quiet in her mother's arms. Mahender sat next to Suniti and held her hand, "I am sorry dear, I couldn't reach on time…" he apologized.

Suniti smiled, "I know you were very busy…don't worry everyone else was here and they looked after me."

Mahender was relieved. He now went out to meet everyone. Suniti held her baby close to her heart as tears rolled down her cheeks. She started feeding her. She was a proud mother now.

Suniti was released from the nursing home the next day.

Chanda was indeed Goddess Lakshmi. Immediately after she was born, Mahender got a promotion. He became the senior manager. He was very happy. He now had more responsibilities, so he started spending more time in the office. He also bought a second-hand car on the advice of his colleagues. How could a senior manager ride a scooter to the office!

Suniti was happy too. Now she didn't have to travel on a scooter.

Suniti wanted to visit her parents in their car, during the weekend. Mahender didn't have time. She asked him a couple of times, but he kept delaying. The car was just like Mahender, only went to the office and came back and went nowhere else. Suniti was visibly upset. Mahender's mother suggested that Suniti should start working again to keep herself busy and she would look after Chanda. His sister was in the final year of studies at college and didn't contribute much towards the housework.

Suniti soon got a job in a local primary school and made new friends. While she was away at school, Mahender's mother and sister looked after Chanda. Chanda built a special bond with her aunty over a period of time.

Chanda was growing up very fast. She started going to school, the same school where Suniti was a teacher.

Life got very monotonous. Everybody led their lives independently. Suniti realised that the connection between her and Mahender was missing. She wanted to go on a holiday, but

Mahender was too busy with work. Suniti wanted Mahender to spend more time with her, but that didn't happen. She would sometimes feel let down and ignored.

The Midlife Crisis

Mahender's parents were getting old. They could not help Suniti with any of her daily chores. They in fact needed attention and assistance. Suniti had to do all the housework and also complete her school duties. She was finding it very difficult to balance her work and house duties. And life in general and the burden of responsibilities.

One day Suniti was alone, sitting in the staff room at school. A senior teacher Mrs. Gupta, a good friend of hers, walked in. She came up to Suniti and said, "All the teachers have been watching you for some time now, you seem very worried and not happy. Tell me, how is life?"

Suniti wanted to avoid talking, but Mrs. Gupta would not let her go without knowing what was wrong with her. She asked again *"Kya hua suniti? Mujhe batao.* (What happened? tell me!), I am like your elder sister."

Suniti broke down in tears, "Mrs. Gupta, I have this feeling that he is getting away from me. We are kind of drifting apart. He doesn't listen to anything I say."

Suniti told her everything.

"Talk to him, I am sure, it is just like any other couple with midlife crisis."

"But how Mrs. Gupta? *Wo mujhse dhang se baat bhi nahi kartey.* (He doesn't even talk to me properly.)"

"Kabhi kabhi ghee nikalne ke liye ungli tedhi karni padti hai – ye to suna hoga. (Bend your finger if you want to get

clarified butter out of a bottle – you must have heard this.)" Suniti nodded her head with a "yes".

"But you wouldn't have heard that, if *ghee* (butter) becomes too hard, you have to warm the bottle to get the butter out smoothly and if it still doesn't come out shake the bottle hard, Understood?" Mrs. Gupta said with a wink.

Suniti's brain was working fast on what to do next.

Mrs. Gupta continued, "Take control of your life Suniti, remember, he might be the boss in the office but at home, you are the boss."

That night, Suniti tried talking to Mahender. "You don't care for me anymore," she said.

"What made you think so? Is it because I didn't take you to your parent's house? We will go sometime next week." Mahender turned to the other side.

"We didn't go out anywhere after our honeymoon. Shall we go to a hill station? I know you love the hills… I think both of us need a break!" Suniti suggested.

"I can't afford to have a break now because it is the financial closing time why don't you go and visit your parents for a few days?" Mahender was snoring in deep sleep before Suniti could say anything more. She was sad and angry.

One day, one of Mahender's friends Rajesh, came home to invite them for the inauguration of his sweet shop. "*Bhabiji,* please come with the entire family. I would highly appreciate your presence and blessings. Please also bring *uncleji* and *auntyji* (Mahender's parents)."

Rajesh and Mahender grew up in the same locality. Mahender was always jealous of Rajesh. He thought Rajesh was smarter, more handsome and always had more money to spend. While Mahender would struggle to talk to girls, Rajesh had a girlfriend in school.

On the inauguration day, the whole family visited the shop. They all got a red-carpet welcome. They were received by Rajesh at the entrance. It was a big business with a large investment. Suniti for a moment thought, she should have married a *halwai* (sweet shop owner) rather than a banker. But all she could do was smile at herself. Everybody else in the party looked so much happier and wealthier than her.

They came back home late and didn't talk, even though Suniti had a lot to talk that night. She felt frustrated with her life and wanted to do something about it, but she wasn't sure how to approach the problem. She was scared.

The Romantic Surprise

One Saturday afternoon, Suniti was sitting alone in the drawing room, watching her favourite family drama on television. The in-laws and Chanda had gone for a pre-marriage celebration of one of the distant relatives, living on the other side of town. She worked out a plan.

At around 8pm, she called Mahender's desk. A couple of calls went unanswered. Suniti was angry. Mahender was sitting at his desk and knew it was Suniti. He just wanted to finish an important assignment. Like every other time, he ignored her calls.

Mahender's colleague, who was sitting at the adjacent table, received a call on his desk. As the phone rang, he turned towards Mahender and said, "*Bhabiji* (sis-in-law – Mahender's wife) is calling I think, shall I answer?"

Mahender asked his friend to pick up the phone and tell her that he was busy in a meeting and would call her back after he returned from the meeting.

His friend did exactly what Mahender told him. He picked up the phone, pretending to not know who was calling, and answered, "Hello, Suresh speaking, how may I help you?"

Suniti replied, "Hello Suresh, it's me, Suniti, Mahender's wife."

"Oh *bhabiji,* how are you?"

"I am fine *bhaisaab* (brother), Where is Mahender? I tried calling him but didn't get any reply."

"He is actually in a meeting with the boss. The moment he comes back I will ask him to give you a call. Is that OK?"

"Yes, that would be fine. Just tell him that I am going to call him in 5 min, it's very urgent. If he doesn't pick up my call, he will regret for the rest of his life," Suniti said with a serious tone and disconnected the phone.

"You are in trouble boss!" Suresh said, turning towards Mahender. "Pick up your phone. *Bhabiji* is not happy. She will call in 5 minutes and if you don't pick up her call you would be in big trouble. She sounded really serious."

Now Mahender was very stressed and worried. He wanted to call Suniti back, but he didn't. Those 5 minutes, felt like 5 hours.

Finally, Mahender's phone rang.

Mahender picked up the phone without any delay, "Sorry Suniti, I was in a meeting. Had to go through an important file. Suresh told me that you called. Yes, what happened? Tell me!"

Suniti continued with a firm voice, "Listen very carefully as I will not repeat my words." Mahender was surprised to hear Suniti talk in such a firm voice, she was always soft spoken.

She continued, "There is going to be hot sex in our bedroom."

"What?" asked Mahender.

"Yes, you heard it right, there will be hot sex in our bedroom, and I am sure I will be there."

"Have you gone mad, what are you talking about?" shouted Mahender.

"Yes, you heard it right. I am going to wait for you till 9 pm."

"What do you mean? What will happen after that?"

"And then I am going to order spicy noodles from Lotus flower restaurant. You know what, they have just started free home delivery."

Mahender got the shock of his life. He asked, "Is that Rajesh's new restaurant? You can't be serious!" Suniti kept quiet.

He had never heard Suniti talk with such a firm voice that too about having sex. There was something seriously wrong somewhere. He looked at his watch. It was 8.30pm.

"But it's 8.30, I can't be home in half an hour."

"Well, that is not my problem," said Suniti and banged the phone down.

Mahender tried calling Suniti, but she was in no mood to talk. Mahender was stressed and was starting to sweat.

"What happened?" Suresh was curious. Mahender just wasn't able to explain the whole conversation. "I don't know what is wrong with her!" he said.

Mahender left all his files on his table, he asked Suresh to organise his table after he was gone. "Why are you rushing?" he asked.

"I have to reach home before 9. Suniti is going to order dinner at 9 pm and I got to reach before that," replied Mahender.

Suresh smiled, "Oh ho! Romantic dinner. You are so lucky!"

"Lucky my foot!" thought Mahender but didn't say anything.

He was sweating profusely. He ran to the car park. Got into his old car and started driving. He kept on looking at his watch as he drove. The car wasn't as fast as he wanted it to be. That day, he felt the need, "hmm I need a new car." He kept pushing the pedal as hard as he could, but the car was too slow for the occasion.

Mahender reached home at 9.30 pm. He parked his car and ran towards the entrance of his house. He saw a man standing just outside the main door of his house. "*Tu kon hai? Yaha kya kar raha hai?* (Who are you? What are you doing here)?"

He replied "*Ji mai Lotus restaurant se delivery karne aya hu* (I am from Lotus restaurant; I am here to deliver the food.) Madam had asked me to wait outside the house."

Mahender smiled, "How much?"

He said, "Four hundred."

Mahender gave him 5, 100-rupee notes and asked him to keep 100 as his tip."

He pointed his finger towards the hat the man was wearing and continued, "*aur tera wo topi mujhe de de* (And give me your hat) I will return it tomorrow."

Mahender took the food packet from him and knocked the door. Suniti opened the door. Without wasting any time, he started, "Are you mad? I almost had a heart attack! What's wrong with you?"

Suniti stood at the door smiling at him. She looked like a fairy, wearing a beautiful gown and had a halo of flowers on her head. As he cooled down, Suniti held his hand and said, "Come in my delivery man."

There was very little lighting, and he couldn't see much. Mahender looked around, "Where is everybody?"

"They have all gone to aunty's daughter's wedding. Tonight, it's just you and me at home." Suniti replied with a wink. "Why didn't you go with them?" Mahender was curious.

"What's the point in my going alone without you? I pretended to be sick. The night is ours," she said with a naughty smile.

Mahender was stunned. He never thought in his wildest of dreams that Suniti had a romantic side too! He understood Suniti had played a prank with him, just to spend the night with him. He took her in his arms. Suniti hugged him tight and cried silently.

Mahender realized he had lost many moments of bliss already because he didn't put any effort into their relationship. They sat close to each other and had a candlelight dinner. Mahender whispered, "The Chinese noodles are hot and spicy, but you look hotter."

Suniti said, "Can I tell you something?"

Mahender acted like a hero "Anything my love... I am all yours!"

"I have never heard you say 'I love you" to me. Not even once!" She said.

Mahender smiled and hugged her tight. She continued "I know ours was an arranged marriage! I was given away to you and asked to love! I was your duty but not love…"

"It's not completely true because according to me, duty is an expression of love! Truly speaking I failed to nurture my love and that's why it took me three long years to finally fall in love. I love you, Suniti!" Mahender laughed at his foolishness.

"I love you very much." whispered Suniti in his ears.

They talked for hours. Last time that they talked so much was probably during their honeymoon. Mahender was enjoying the night and realised what he had been missing for so many years. They never really made an effort to come so close and challenge each other's emotions. Mahender whispered pointing at the bedside lamp, "Let me turn the lights off."

Suniti whispered back, "nope, let them be on and why are we whispering? There is nobody else in the house. Just you and me."

They needed some sleep. The bedside lamps were turned off, only to be turned back on again after some time.

The lights did turn on and off, a couple of times that night.

Suniti woke up next morning to a knock on the door. She had slept in. It was 8 am. She couldn't find Mahender. He had probably gone for his hockey practice. She opened the door, and everybody walked in.

"*Function kaisi thi* (How was the function)?" asked Suniti

Her mother-in-law replied "*achi thi, thak gaye hum sab* (good. We are all tired)."

Mahender returned home after some time.

Mahender made a few changes in his life to keep a balance between work and home. He bought a new car. He tried hard to come home on time to help out Suniti with her housework. He spent quality time with his family. He also took everyone out occasionally.

Meanwhile, Mahender's sister's marriage was fixed. Mahender and Suniti had a big role to play during the event. Mahender tried to help his father as much as he could, financially. Suniti chose a beautiful *lehnga* (bridal dress) for her and managed all the wedding arrangements. The family was full of praise for her. It was a big wedding and attended by all their relatives, Mahender's office colleagues and close neighbours.

Mahender and everybody in the family, appreciated Suniti's input. The wedding celebrations went well and after Vidai, Mahender's sister went to her husband's house. Chanda started missing her aunt very much. There was nobody to play with or tell her stories. At times, she would get cranky and cry for no reason.

Mahender's parents took this opportunity and suggested that it was time for Chanda to get a little brother whom she could play with. Suniti didn't respond but Mahender replied saying Chanda could play with her grandparents, till they became financially stable.

Mahender's office colleagues met Suniti during his sister's marriage. They liked her friendly behaviour and started inviting her to their parties. Mahender had never taken Suniti to any office parties. He was not sure of Suniti's public persona or communication skills. But after the way she communicated with everybody at his sister's wedding, he was confident that she would fit in very nicely.

He started taking Suniti to all the office parties.

Suniti also very much enjoyed accompanying her husband to the parties. She had started taking an interest in Mahender's work.

Soon Mahender got another promotion. This time his colleagues congratulated Suniti also and gave credit to her for Mahender's success in his career. Suniti was very proud.

Suddenly, Suniti became very busy. Everybody started inviting her and Mahender to their parties and private dinners. Suniti needed more *sarees*. She couldn't wear the same *saree* twice. After all she was the Boss's wife. At the parties, the ladies were very critical about others' dresses and jewellery and often formed opinions. Suniti had to be careful about choosing her *sarees* and jewellery. She borrowed a few *sarees* from her mother and mother-in-law and somehow managed the show.

With his promotion, Mahender had again become very busy in office. He again started returning home very late and family outings eventually stopped. Suniti was getting worried and sometimes a bit irritated too. She sometimes wondered if keeping their relationship intact was only her responsibility. Mahender didn't care much! Suniti had learnt to compromise with the situation.

Chapter 3

Learning

Everything was well and life was crawling along. All hell broke loose after Chanda's fifth birthday party celebrations. That evening all their friends and relatives were invited. Mahender had promised that he would join them, but he decided to stay back late at office. Suniti was very embarrassed. Everyone was expecting Mahender to be there. They kept asking about him. Suniti had no answer. She called Mahender a couple of times, but she didn't get an answer. Some of the guests had started whispering about their relationship. Suniti was very upset. "For once, couldn't he have come home on time?" she asked herself.

Suniti didn't talk to Mahender that night. Mahender tried to explain to her that he had overseas guests, but she felt he was making excuses.

Next morning Mahender tried to ease the situation. "Chanda, ask your mother to forgive me for the last time please." He told Chanda hoping Suniti would hear him.

"No! You can't get away with it every time. It was so embarrassing, having to clarify to everybody in the party about why you were not there. Everybody had their own theories!"

Mahender tried to pacify her, "I am extremely sorry. It won't happen again."

Suniti wasn't stopping "You know what? You lied…you don't need a family…you don't love anyone. You only love yourself and your work"

"What are you saying? I work day and night for my family. I want to give you all comfort in life!"

Disagreement (Hell Breaks Loose)

"And have you been successful in doing that Mr. Mahendra Pratap Singh? No! Your juniors have bigger cars than you. Their wives wear new *sarees* and jewellery at every party. Each year they take their families to Europe for holidays…what have you done?" She burst out in anger.

"You know very well I have more liabilities. I have too many loans to pay. I can't take any risk with my work and have never taken any favours from any of my clients!" Mahender raised his voice.

"Don't shout, you are not the only one who has spent on a sister's marriage or a brother's education… The whole world looks after old parents, but they also love their wife and children. This was Chanda's fifth birthday! What memories will Chanda grow up with? Thank God she doesn't remember that her father was not there to welcome her when she first came into this world! He was in his office attending a meeting." Suniti mocked at him. Mahender was quiet all the while but now he lost it.

Mahender lost his temper. "How will you know about meetings? You are just an ordinary primary teacher. You work and leave as and when you like! Well, you can afford to do that because you don't have to pay back any loan or monthly bills like me. So, you can only complain! Have you ever thought of contributing and helping your husband?"

Mahender's parents heard everything and tried to intervene, but they were in no mood to listen. Things got from bad to worse.

"No… I didn't. My priority was my child, my home and your old parents. If you wanted help, you could have asked my father during marriage. He would have loved to give his son-in law a fortune! Why did you act so innocent then?" The argument went out of control and anger took over. They were not thinking straight. Mahender, in the heat of anger, raised his hand to hit Suniti and then stopped.

Suniti was shocked to see Mahender. She never thought he could raise his hand on anyone! She stood frozen.

Mahender realised it was a mistake. He was feeling guilty. But Suniti's words stung like a bee. She had pushed him too far. Without taking the fight any further, he left the room.

After work, Mahender returned home in the evening. He had got some snacks and sweets and thought he would apologise to Suniti. He was feeling very bad after what happened. His mother opened the door. He couldn't see Suniti anywhere. Even Chanda was nowhere to be seen!

"Is Chanda still sleeping?" He asked his mother. His mother looked very annoyed.

"No… I think by this time she must be playing with her cousins in her grandfather's house." She said sarcastically.

"What do you mean?" Mahender was taken by surprise

"Suniti has left this house with Chanda because you raised your hand. I couldn't stop her. I feel ashamed of you Mahender." His mother said, disappointed.

Life just went on. Their ego stopped them from talking to each other. Both realised it was a mistake but waited for the other to make the first call.

Lesson Learnt

Time just flew. It was a little over one-year Mahender and Suniti were living separately. Time had taken its toll. Slowly their ego was overshadowed by repentance. Mahender wanted to get Suniti back in his life but didn't have the courage to tell her. Suniti also wanted to come back but she was waiting for Mahender to make the first move.

Though they were separate, Suniti kept in touch with Mahender's parents and sister. She also sent Chanda to meet her grandparents regularly during the weekends with her brother. Mahender started staying at home during weekends to meet Chanda.

Chanda became the common point of communication. Both Mahender and Suniti would ask little Chanda about each other. Mahender came to know that Suniti was thinking seriously about her career and got herself admitted to a part time MBA degree course. He understood; it was all the aftermath of their fight. Sunita was out to prove herself. Mahender felt guilty but at the same time, felt happy that Suniti was fulfilling her long lost dream!

Mahender's father didn't take his son's separation very well. He didn't talk much, was always sad and stressed. One day while in office Mahender got a call. His father had a heart attack. Mahender reached home as soon as he could. A local doctor was attending his father and the ambulance was on its way. He was soon transferred to the Emergency at the nearest hospital. His father was put on life support. Mahender's sister came to meet him. Suniti was also informed. She came as soon as she could.

Mahender's mother hugged her and cried her heart out. Mahender was touched to see that. He never expected their bonding was so strong. The next morning Mahender's father passed away. Mahender did all their duties with great care and respect.

Mahender arranged a prayer meeting in his father's memory. All relatives and friends came to pay their respects for the departed soul. Suniti also came with Chanda. Mahender's mother was very touched to see them. His sister welcomed her and made her comfortable. Chanda ran and sat on her father's lap. Relatives whispered and exchanged glances. Some were happy, while some found reasons to gossip. Suniti didn't bother about them much. She carried out her duties of being the daughter-in-law of the family. Along with Mahender she paid tributes to her father-in-law, fed the priests and distributed food and clothes to the poor as customary.

Mahender took a quick glance or two, at Suniti, "That gentle smile on her lips is missing. She doesn't look happy." he thought.

Suniti thought, "He is looking thinner. He must be missing his daughter very much."

The invisible bond was pulling them together. They still cared for each other. Circumstances were keeping them away. After the condolence meeting was over, Suniti called for Chanda. It was time to go. Chanda wanted to stay with her father for some more time.

Mahender didn't want to lose this opportunity. He quietly walked close to Suniti and said," Can we make a new beginning?

I am sorry Suniti. Please come back home. I can't live without you." Suniti looked at Mahender.

She didn't want to lose this opportunity either. She wasn't going to give it away so easily. "Come next Sunday, my parents wanted to spend some time with you. We will have lunch and we will come back home." she said.

Before Mahender could say anything, she turned to Chanda and said, "Let's go today, Chanda. We will come back next Sunday. Papa will come to take us!"

Mahender's mother was observing them very closely and was very happy. She looked at Mahender's father's picture and thought, "*Kash aap jinda hotey ye dekhne ke liye* (I wish they got together while you were still here to see it.)"

Got Together

On the Sunday, Mahender reached Suniti's father's house on time. He was a little unsure of what Suniti's parents thought about the whole thing. But they welcomed him warmly as always. He spent the day and returned home in the evening with his wife and daughter.

Suniti was not the same as before. She had become quiet. She communicated to him only when required. She kept herself busy in the daily chores and Chanda's education. Mahender wanted to spend time with her and go for outings, but she would always give some excuse. She would go to bed late at night after Mahender fell asleep.

Mahender understood that the wounds of separation hadn't healed completely. Suniti hadn't forgiven him yet! Mahender wanted the old Suniti back in his life. The new Suniti was very cold and disconnected. The warmth was missing.

He thought hard and decided to ask about her on-going MBA and help her in completing the course. That was the only way he could win back Suniti's confidence.

One day, after everybody had their dinner, Mahender came and sat next to Chanda in the sitting room. Suniti was in the kitchen doing her chores. "I will tell you a very interesting story," he said looking at Suniti from the corner of his eyes.

"Story hmmm," thought Chanda. Mahender wanted the full attention of both daughter and mother.

"Is it a story of a tiger or an elephant?' Chanda asked with excitement.

Mahender smiled, after a brief pause, he continued, "Not really a tiger or elephant but something more real. It's about a parrot."

"A real story papa?" Chanda was curious.

"Well, you can decide that after you hear the story!" Mahender looked at Suniti. She had stopped her work but as soon as she saw Mahender looking at her, she continued working. Mahender understood Suniti was listening to the story too.

After taking a big breath, he continued, "Once upon a time, there lived a parrot called *Mithu* (meaning sweet). She was beautiful. She had shinning green wings, a long feathery tail and a bright orange beak. She was a pet in a rich *zamindar's* (landlord) house. The landlord had got Mithu for his son on his fifth birthday. Do you know that parrots can say or utter words that are often used or taught to them?"

"Yes, I know, parrots are intelligent birds," Chanda answered.

"The little boy taught the parrot some basic words – Good Morning in the mornings and Good Night before going to bed. Every time Mithu uttered those words, she was given her favourite red chilli as a treat. The boy had many friends and every time his friends visited him, he would show-off with Mithu. He would either ask him to say Good Morning or Good Night. The same set of words."

Chanda commented, "Oh that must have been really boring for Mithu, saying the same words over and over again?"

"Yes, Mithu was getting a bit frustrated. She could actually say lot more words than just morning and evening."

"Why did the boy not teach her more words?" Chanda asked.

"The boy probably thought that Mithu was not capable enough!" Mahender looked at Suniti. She had stopped her work and was listening to the story."

"I think that's very cruel."

"I know. The parrot was very smart, and she had learnt lot more by listening to others in the house. She could speak complete sentences. But there was no incentive for her to say any more than those two greetings."

"As time passed Mithu got older. Now she could tell stories and recite poems, but no one paid any attention. Nobody really valued Mithu's creativity. She lived in the cage, spoke the two words and got the red chillies."

"At least she got red chillies. Some parrots don't even get that!!" Suniti said suddenly. Mahender had broken the ice. Suniti was talking. He continued his story with more enthusiasm.

"Soon Mithu got very frustrated. She started thinking about flying out of the cage and being free"

"Wow what a daring bird! Then what happened papa?" Asked Chanda.

Mahender smiled and continued. "But then she loved her master very much. She didn't want to hurt him, so she carried on with her boring life. One day, there was a *Kavi Sammelan* (gathering of poets for poetry recital) organised at the *Zamindar's* house. Lots of writers came from all over the country and recited poems. *Mithu* listened to all their recitals. He also wanted to recite a poem. She asked her master for his permission. The boy got very angry. How could a parrot who said only two words dare to recite a poem in front of such great writers? He shouted at *Mithu* for the first time in his life. *Mithu* was very hurt." Mahender stopped and looked at Suniti. She was facing the other side and was crying silently.

"Then what happened papa? Did Mithu fly away?" asked Chanda.

"Yes, she did otherwise how would she follow her dreams?"

"That's nice but how did *Mithu* open the cage?" Chanda interrupted.

"It took a little time. *Mithu* was a clever bird. She observed that every morning when the maid opened the cage door to give her some seeds and vegetables, she just closed the door but didn't lock it. She would then get some water and pour it for *Mithu* and then lock the door. She was very confident that Mithu wouldn't fly. Mithu observed the maid for a few days and then one day when the maid went to get water, Mithu took the flight to freedom."

Chanda was very happy. She was sleepy too. Soon she fell asleep.

There was silence in the room for some time.

"Did Mithu realize her dreams?" Suniti asked turning to her husband.

"I don't know but I will help my Mithu to realize her dreams for sure." Mahender walked to Suniti and embraced her. He stroked her hair as she cried.

Chapter 4

Honesty

Suniti was an educated and forward – looking girl who could take her own decisions but couldn't follow her dreams because of family restrictions. Marrying Mahender was her decision even though theirs was a business family. She preferred a smart English-speaking professional rather than a traditional businessman. But after her marriage she realized she got everything she wished for except two things, her husband's time and enough money.

Suniti worked hard to get her husband's time and attention. She managed to change him using her beauty and intelligence. She even separated from him to teach him a lesson. After their brief separation, Mahender realised her importance and started spending more time with her. But as far as money was concerned Suniti was not so lucky!

She was tired of Mahender's habit of calculating money for everything. She wanted Chanda to go to a good private school, but they couldn't afford it. She had to admit her to the neighbourhood school where she taught. They didn't have any help at home for household work. She had to share all the work with Mahender's mother. Mahender drove a small car and they have always had to hire a taxi if they ever went to a function with Mahender's parents. Suniti wanted to buy a bigger car, but they never could save enough money for that.

All of Mahender's work colleagues had big cars and went for expensive holidays. Their wives wore expensive jewellery and *sarees* to the office parties. She was the odd one out. She had a very limited collection of *sarees* and jewellery, and she would have to repeat them with caution. She didn't want to give the impression that she wore the same *saree* on many occasions. Mahender's colleagues had air conditioners in every room, but Suniti had only one in the living room!

One day while having dinner, Suniti asked, "*Ek bat puchu*? (May I ask a question?)"

"*Pucho*! (Yes ask!)

"I was actually wanting to ask you this question for a long time. How can your work colleagues afford big cars and lavish lifestyles? I thought their pay grades were very similar to yours. We have had the small old car for so many years now." Mahender was quiet. He didn't have an answer.

After a brief pause Mahender said, "I honestly don't have an answer for your questions. I do my best to the best of my ability."

Suniti completed her MBA with support from Mahender and his mother. She had worked hard and come out with flying colours. She had thought her entry into the corporate world would provide her the luxuries that she always wanted to have. But that didn't happen.

Although she got offers from many big companies around the country, she had to choose a job in her own city that was not too demanding. She had to compromise on her pay package though. It was quite frustrating for her, but family was her first priority. She accepted it as her fate.

After she took up the job Suniti made a few changes in their lifestyle. She started earning well but, their lifestyle was still not comparable to Mahender's colleagues. All of them seemed to have a magic wand!

Soon after Suniti completed one year in her job, she fell pregnant. Mahender's mother was very happy and so was Chanda. Mahender again wished for a boy, but he didn't mention it to Suniti this time. Suniti was happy too, but she wished she would get her annual pay rise before their office came to know of her pregnancy.

It was Suniti's birthday. Mahender got home early with flowers and a gift. Suniti was very surprised. In all the eight years of their marriage, Mahender had never remembered any birthdays or anniversaries. She was happy that Mahender was responding to her expectations. She opened the gift and was flabbergasted. Mahender got her a shining gold necklace. It was adorned by lots of red and green stones! He also got a matching silk *saree*.

"Wow this is so lovely. Thank you so much!" said Suniti and walked into her bedroom and Mahender followed. Suniti sat in front of her dressing table and tried her new necklace. She draped the *saree* over her body. "How do I look?" she asked. "Excellent" he replied.

She looked very happy. Mahender was relieved, "Thank god, she likes it." he thought.

He said "beautiful…wear this for Chaudhary's daughter's wedding."

"When is it? You never mentioned anything about a wedding. So, they finally found a boy? What does the boy do?" Suniti asked the questions in a row.

"I don't know exactly. The boy has some business." Mahender said.

"That means he has a lot of money!" Suniti commented. "So, you got this necklace for wearing in Chaudhary's daughter's wedding…right?"

"Not really… I got the gift for your birthday…but…you always say you don't have enough jewellery or *sarees* to wear, and you dread going to my office parties. So, I bought them. I know this is not very expensive, but it looks good on you." Mahender managed to answer to Suniti's satisfaction.

"To me, this is extraordinary," smiled Suniti as she looked at herself in the mirror. Mahender smiled.

On the day of Mr. Chaudhary's daughter's wedding Mahender came home a bit early. Suniti dressed up well for the occasion. She wore the new necklace set and the *saree*. She looked gorgeous. She got compliments from her mother-in-law and Chanda.

Mahender opened the car door for Suniti. She held Mahender's arm as he drove. They were the happiest couple in the whole world. Suniti looked very cheerful while going for a party. Finally, she could show off her jewellery and the new *saree* to the other ladies.

"Who said money can't buy happiness!!" Mahender thought to himself.

They arrived at a five-star hotel, the venue for the wedding party. Mahender's colleague Mr. Chaudhary had money and good taste. So, he had arranged everything perfectly. There was an overload of opulence and glamour.

The wedding was being held at the hotel lawns. At the entrance everyone was greeted with a rose and sprinkling of rosewater. Mr. and Mrs. Chaudhary stood there welcoming their guests. The bride and the groom were seated on a podium decorated with flowers. Mahender and Suniti walked up to the podium and had to walk up a couple of steps. Mahender held Suniti's hand. She was in the third month of her pregnancy and needed to be careful with her steps. She appreciated Mahender's attention. They congratulated the bride and the groom. Suniti handed over an envelope with a gift cheque and wished them a happy married life.

The photographer requested them to stand for a photo opportunity. As they walked down the steps, Suniti held Mahender's hand in her own. She was feeling special. Suniti whispered, "Did you see Mrs. Chaudhary was staring at my necklace!" Mahender's face lit up with a gleaming smile. It didn't really matter to him, but he finally knew the secret of keeping Suniti happy.

It was time to socialise. They walked up to the group of people who were close colleagues of Mahender. Everybody in the group greeted them. The waiter got them drinks. Suniti knew most of the women there. They all complimented her. A few even wanted to see her necklace closely. Suniti was feeling very proud. She had to admit that her husband had made a good choice.

Amongst all the familiar faces, there stood an unfamiliar, attractive and handsome looking man in his late forties. He stood with a few of his friends a little away from the entrance. He was very loud and outspoken. He knew how to make his presence felt. Suniti was seeing him for the first time. "Hmm he must be special" she thought.

Soon Mahender walked up to him and introduced Suniti to him. "Meet Mr. and Mrs. Shekhar Sharma, one of our most premium clients. He is a much-respected businessman. He owns a number of businesses."

Suniti wished him and his wife with folded hands and smiled. Shekhar also greeted her back. Then he laughed aloud. "Don't embarrass me Mr. Singh, I am not the owner. Your bank owns it! I still owe a lot of money to your bank. But let me tell you, I am ever grateful to your bank for helping me reach where I am today!" Suniti was impressed. She had never imagined a successful businessman to be so humble!

Suniti and a few of the ladies settled around a table. Sitting there, Suniti could easily see Mr. and Mrs. Sharma standing with his friends and talking. Suniti noticed that Mr. Sharma knew all of Mahender's colleagues very well and they knew him too. None of them would go past without wishing him. He greeted them back with a pleasant smile. They would briefly talk to him and his wife and then move on. Suniti couldn't help but observe an interesting pattern. After they finished their conversation with each of them, they moved on to meet the bride and groom. Mr. and Mrs. Sharma would talk among themselves and burst out with laughter. Suniti was very curious. Mr. Sharma was quite loud, so Suniti didn't have to make much effort. She just had to switch off from the gossip of the ladies and concentrate on Mr. Sharma's conversation without directly looking at them or making any eye contact. She was eavesdropping.

One of Mahender's colleagues walked in with his wife. Mr. Sharma greeted him with a warm smile. After a brief conversation, as they moved on, he said, "Did you see the expensive watch he was wearing and his wife's bracelet? I gave both as Diwali gifts. He approved two of my projects. I also sponsored his holiday to Hawai last summer!"

"Isn't he the senior manager?" Asked one of his friends. "Yes! Senior or Junior everyone needs money! Remember… money brings more money!" Everybody else in his group agreed and appreciated Mr. Sharma's wisdom.

Suniti couldn't believe her ears. She smiled after hearing Mr. Sharma's comments and waited for the next entrant. She wanted to know what Mr. Sharma thought of other bankers. After a brief pause another gentleman walked in with his wife. He greeted him and talked about different things. As he moved on Mr. Sharma whispered, "This one is an Assistant General Manager. Did you see his wife's gold necklace set? I gifted it to her on their anniversary. I also gave them *two lakh rupees* (two hundred thousand rupees) to get their house renovated." His friends were surprised again. And this time they shared a hearty laugh. All the secrets were coming out and Mr. Sharma wasn't holding back. Suniti's opinion about the bank managers was changing.

The story continued for a few more people who walked in. She knew her husband was honest, and she could have never guessed this secret path to a lavish lifestyle and big holidays. It was an eye-opener for her. She was now aware of it all.

Suniti was curious though. She wanted to know what Mr. Sharma would say if Mahender walked through that entrance. But he was busy with his friends. She had a brilliant idea. She went up to Mahender and said, "Can you please get my shawl from the car? It's getting a bit chilly."

She wanted Mahender to walk out of that door, get the shawl and walk back in through that entrance. Mr. Sharma wouldn't miss him for sure.

Mahender was in the middle of a conversation, "I will get it in 5 mins," he said. Suniti nodded and she went back to her place at the table. After finishing the conversation Mahender went out to get Suniti's shawl from the car.

Her focus was on the entrance. Her heart was beating fast. She was hoping to hear what she believed was true about Mahender.

After a few minutes Suniti saw Mahender walking in. To her dismay Mahender wasn't walking alone. He must have met their General Manager outside and he was walking in with him and his wife. He was a lot more senior than Mahender. Mr. Sharma greeted both warmly and started to converse. Mahender was in a hurry to give Suniti her shawl and get back to his own conversations. He didn't wait for Mr. Sharma to talk to him, he just waved at him and came to Suniti.

Suniti was disheartened. Her plan had failed. But she kept her ears open.

Mr. Sharma spoke to the general manager for quite some time. He introduced his friends to him. As he left Mr. Sharma said, "This General Manager is very influential. Whatever he recommends is generally approved by the board. He only approves large projects. He is a bit expensive. He loves to visit Paris every year, with his wife. We sponsor his trips every year. Did you see the expensive jewellery his wife was wearing?" His friends nodded. He continued, "I gifted her last year. Not just that, I have gifted his wife many things and if I decide to take it all back, she will have nothing to wear." He said with a wink and a big grin. His friends had a hearty laugh.

Suniti was eavesdropping on the conversation as she wrapped the shawl around herself. She was a bit disappointed.

She had lost a golden opportunity to hear what he thought about Mahender.

Mr. Sharma continued "Did you see the other gentleman who entered with him, the one who had a shawl in his hand? He is Mahender Pratap Singh. He is a senior manager at the bank."

Suniti didn't move. She sat there like a stone. She didn't want to miss even a single word of what Mr. Sharma was saying.

He continued "He is the most honest banker that I have seen and met in my life. If you submit a good feasible project proposal, he will approve it without any hesitation. But if you submit a bad project which he thinks isn't good, he will never approve it, even if you give him a million dollars. I have tried offering him jewellery for his wife and holidays, he is just not interested."

Suniti had tears in her eyes. She had always been so critical about Mahender's financial situation and compared him with his colleagues. She was shocked and felt somewhat ashamed. She realized that Mahender had the real wealth which was his Honesty! And that's why nobody dared to talk bad about Mahender behind his back. He was a real Hero.

Suniti held her head high, even though her lifestyle was not as lavish as the others. She didn't have a holiday every year, but she was a proud wife. It was getting late, and she had an early morning meeting the following day. She came to Mahender and said, "We better get home. Got work tomorrow."

As they walked out of the venue, Mr. Sharma said goodbye and asked, "Hope you liked the food, and the arrangements were up to your expectations!" Suniti understood the gesture. She smiled and they left the venue as Mahender waved goodbye.

On their way back, Mahender was extra careful. He had had a couple of drinks. Suniti was quiet as if she was in deep thought. Mahender was confused. The whole evening, she had looked so happy. What happened now? He was curious and asked, "You don't look very happy now? What happened? Aren't you feeling well?"

Suniti smiled and said, "Don't worry I am fine. In fact, I have never felt better before." Mahender was even more confused.

Suniti continued, "Thank god, you didn't listen to me." Mahender was surprised. He thought he had started listening to Suniti and did things as she wished.

She continued, "I am sorry for all that I have said to you. Do you know Chaudhary's party today was arranged by your premier client Shekhar Sharma…? And the necklace that Verma's wife wore, was given by Shekhar Sharma on her anniversary…and…"

"I know all this Suniti. You have come to know about it today. It's okay, let others do what they think is right." Mahender said.

Suniti now had nothing more to say. She just said, "You know what? I have realized one thing today. Honesty is something very few people can handle. You can't expect it from everyone. And for that you need a special power which God has given to you! We actually have been blessed with the most expensive gift."

Tears rolled down her cheeks as Mahender drove home.

Chapter 5

Hope

Mahender and Suniti's life was now more settled. They had learnt some of the most important lessons of life. They never lost hope in their troubled times.

After realising the truth behind the affluent life of Mahendra's colleagues, Suniti changed her view about money and felt proud of Mahender. She now believed that money could buy anything but happiness.

In spite of this, she got caught up in the rat race where she had to choose between money and happiness.

Suniti continued to chase her dreams and got into the corporate world. She worked hard all throughout her pregnancy to get her confirmation. She gave birth to a baby girl. Mahender had learnt to accept things as they came. He wasn't too fussed about the next child being a boy or a girl. He thought the little one was as beautiful as an angel! Chanda was very excited to get a little sister. She named her Tara. Suniti enjoyed life with her family while on a paid maternity leave.

Tara was a six-month-old when Suniti returned to work. Soon life became very busy for her. She struggled to keep a balance between her job and home. Mahender's mother was getting older. She couldn't do as much work as before. Little Tara by then had started crawling. She needed someone to continuously run after her. Chanda also had more studies now and needed help. Mahender had to take leave from his office to prepare Chanda during her school tests. Suniti hired a maid to do all the household work and look after Tara. But things were not going too well. Their home had lost that warmth it had before! Life had become very mechanical, and everyone worked like a machine.

Suniti thought of leaving her job, but Mahender didn't want her to do that. After all she had worked very hard to reach that position. She was enjoying her financial independence and Mahender was afraid that she might be frustrated if she quit her job. Mahender couldn't also ignore the fact that they got used to the money and comfort that came with her job.

Suniti had her own argument though. The pressures of corporate life were putting a lot of stress on her. She wished that she had more than 24 hours in a day. Very often she had to constantly choose between work and home. She believed that if she ran after money and continued working full time, she wouldn't have enough time to spend with her two girls, something she didn't want to compromise on. After much deliberation, she chose family over her work.

Suniti resigned from her corporate job. Everyone including Mahender was very happy. She stayed at home and looked after her girls. Being a part of their growing years, she felt at peace. She would once in a while meet up with her ex-work colleagues. She didn't want to lose that touch.

She realised that teaching was a better option for her. It would give her more time for the family and keep her busy too. Suniti started applying for jobs in schools. By then she was settled and could easily manage her family demands. She was in control. One morning she got a call. It was from a colleague at her previous office. She wanted Suniti to join her NGO which worked for poor and underprivileged children. Suniti was quite excited and discussed this with Mahender who encouraged her to join.

Teaching turned out to be more satisfying than a corporate job. The love that she got from her students could never match the money earned in a corporate job. She had more fun in school among children than with adults who behaved like children.

New Opportunity

Mahender was working on a special project that involved funding by the government and an overseas development fund. One morning, he got a call from a senior manager, he asked him to meet him at his office. He wanted to discuss an assignment with him.

They met the same afternoon and discussed a possible overseas posting for Mahender.

The assignment was a posting in Australia for 2 years. One of the major development banks was looking for a person whose education and experience matched closely with Mahender's background. Mahender promised to get back to the manager after a couple of days. It was a great opportunity, but he wanted to discuss it with Suniti and the kids. He was confused on what to do!

The girls went to good schools, Suniti was happy with her current situation and his mother was old. Upheaving their lives to move to a new country for his sake wouldn't be fair on them.

They would have to start afresh. He even thought of moving alone but was worried, who would look after his family, while he was away?

Mahender walked into the house, disturbed and lost in thought. He had a shower and sat in front of the television, while Suniti was cooking in the kitchen. It was 9.30 pm, time for a very popular family serial on television. Suniti and the girls loved it. Mahender had no interest in family dramas. He thought it was a waste of time. He would usually pick up his newspaper and go to another room.

But that day, things were different. Mahender sat with the family in front of the television without his newspapers. He was watching the serial with everybody else.

Suniti was surprised and asked, "*Is time tum roj bhag jatey ho, aaj kya hua*? (Usually, this time you run away from television, what happened today?) Are you going to watch the serial with us?"

Mahender nodded and replied, "Yes, I will." Suniti was surprised.

As the serial progressed Suniti observed that Mahender was not really watching the television but was in deep thought. After dinner, the girls went to their rooms and Mahender went to his bedroom and lay on bed, relaxing with a magazine. Suniti walked in, "Hey listen, I have been watching you for the past couple of hours, something seems to be bothering you. What is it, tell me?"

Mahender kept the magazine on the bedside table and sat up, "I have a big decision to make, and I don't know how to tell you." Said Mahender.

"Just tell me, don't hold back."

"Listen, there is a new position at a development bank in Australia and my bank wants to put forward my name as a candidate."

Suniti looked worried, she asked, "What will happen to us?"

"What do you mean?"

"If you go overseas and we will be here. How will it all work out?" asked Suniti.

"Are you mad? You are all coming with me. I am just worried about the kids and *Ma*." Said Mahender.

Both the girls were in their teens. Chanda was going to a senior school while Tara went to a middle school.

"I am sure the girls will have their own opinions. You should have told me before that this was coming. This is so sudden; I don't know what to say," Suniti said.

"I also didn't know this. It happened so suddenly after lunch today. One of the senior managers called me to his office and told me this," Mahender said.

They were both silent for a minute.

"Let's not worry too much. We will talk to them tomorrow evening."

Next day, Mahender came back from work early. After having a quick shower, he had a chat with Suniti and decided to talk to his mother first. Mahender's mother was surprised to see him in her room. Normally he didn't enter his parent's room unless there was something important.

"*kya hua beta*? (What happened)?" Said his mother.

"*Mummy apse bat karni thi. Office wale Australia bhej rahe hai.* (I want to talk to you mummy. My office people want to send me to Australia for a job)" said Mahender and sat next to his mother on the bed.

She replied, "*Isme sochna kya hai? Tere liye achcha hai?* (What is there to think? Is it a good opportunity?)"

"*Ha Ma* (yes Ma)," replied Mahender.

"*Fir sochna kya hai? Ha bol de. Hum gaon jake rahe lenge. Waha gandgi kam hai aur sukoon jyada.* (What is there to think? You say yes to them. Don't worry about me. I will go to the village and live there. There is less pollution there and more peace.)." She said.

Suniti was standing right outside the door. She heard the conversation and had tears in her eyes. Mahender walked out of the room.

He looked at Suniti, "Let's have a chat with the girls." They both walked into the living room where the girls were watching television.

"I have secured a new position in Australia! What do you think girls?" said Mahender.

Chanda and Tara looked at each other with excitement.

"Wow papa that sounds great. Can we go after I finish this year, please? I don't want to travel in the middle of the year?" said Chanda

Mahender was happy and said, "Of course, everything will be arranged as per your wishes. Nothing is final yet."

That night Mahender and Suniti discussed in detail late into the night.

Next morning Mahender met his manager and agreed to go ahead.

"So, what is the next step? Do I have to do anything?" Asked Mahender.

"I would request you to submit your latest resume to us. There will be a series of interviews. You will be informed prior to each interview. We have shortlisted five potential candidates for the role. I will send your resume to the HR department of the overseas bank and wait for their response."

Mahender hadn't made a resume in a long time. He tried writing it up and got all confused. He thought of taking Suniti's help.

Both of them were awake till late that night, trying to figure out the best possible resume for Mahender. Mahender picked up a sample resume online and decided to stick with that format.

Next morning Mahender handed over the resume to his manager.

A couple of days later, Mahender was informed that he was among the 3 shortlisted candidates. A telephone interview was going to be organised with one of the overseas managers.

His telephone interview went well, and his manager told him that he would have to appear for a final interview over the phone with the overseas bank selection committee.

Mahender prepared himself for the final interview. On the D Day he put on his best suit and a brand-new tie. He went into the conference room in his office. His interview went very well. But the truth was that his probability of getting the job was only 33%.

He went back home; Suniti was eagerly waiting to know how it went. She asked, "Do you know who the other two are?"

"I don't know, but my gut feeling is Vishal and Sanjeev. Both of them were dressed in their best suits, just like me," Mahender replied with a smile.

Suniti got a bit sad. She said, "Oh, I think Vishal is more qualified than you. He also has more experience."

"Well, we will have to wait and see I guess," replied Mahender.

After about a week, Mahender received a call from one of his senior managers, confirming his selection for the position. His manager asked him to see him at his office that afternoon.

Mahender knocked on his office door and walked into his room, "Welcome and congratulations Mahender. Have a seat." His manager greeted him.

"Thank you, Sir."

"Before we talk, I think we must have a toast for your selection. Hmmm do you want tea or coffee?"

"Tea would be good." said Mahender.

His manager called his helper and asked him to get 2 cups of tea. "We will keep the wine for your farewell party, so today only tea for you." He laughed.

Mahender was smiling and waited for his manager to continue.

"You will be traveling to Australia for the project. Your position is based in Melbourne."

They had a detailed discussion about what to do next. The tea, that day, tasted so much better than any other day. Satisfied with the outcome, Mahender walked out of the room, and he called up Suniti and conveyed the message. She was happy and excited.

Australia sounded fascinating, especially the kangaroos, hockey, cricket and the beaches. Mahender loved Australia from whatever exposure he had watching cricket matches on television.

He came home with a big cake for everybody to celebrate. Suniti was happy but tense at the same time. She was happy for the new opportunity that lay ahead and worried that the new land was totally unknown to her.

Mahender took a couple of days off from work and moved his mother to their village house. He made sure she was comfortable there. She loved moving back to their native village. She would get a chance to live with her extended family. Everyone was keen to help.

Mahender thought he was going for a longer term posting. He wanted to sell their house, but Suniti had emotional attachment to the house, so they decided not to. Suniti was of the opinion that their move was only temporary, and they would come back one day.

The plan was that Mahender would go first and take a house on rent. Suniti and the kids would move at the end of their school year so that there was no disruption to their studies.

Farewell Party

It was Mahender's last week in office. His colleagues had organised a farewell party for him in a five-star hotel.

As Mahender and Suniti walked in, they were greeted by Mahender's Manager, "Welcome *bhabiji,* you look gorgeous and very happy!"

Suniti replied gently with a cheerful, "Thank you."

She couldn't help but notice Mr. Sharma from Mahender's manager's wedding party held earlier in the year. He was standing next to Mahender's manager. He wished with folded hands "*Namashkar bhabiji aur Mahender ji.* Congratulations. (Greetings, sister-in-law and Mahender, congratulations to both of you) Welcome welcome." Mahender smiled back and shook hands with Mr. Sharma.

Suniti smiled at him too. With folded hands she wished "*Namashkar Sharma ji* (Greetings Sharmaji)."

Mr. Sharma was very surprised that she remembered him from the previous party. They only had a brief conversation. "You still remember me *bhabiji*, thank you," said Mr. Sharma.

Suniti replied, "How can I forget you Sharmaji, I learnt a lot from you that night or should I say you taught me a big lesson that night."

"What do you mean?" asked Mr. Sharma.

"I will tell you some other day. Today it's time to celebrate," said Suniti and they walked in. Mr. Sharma stood there welcoming other guests.

Everybody got busy in small groups, laughing, and discussing their fun times in office. From her experience at the last party, Suniti kind of got addicted to all the office gossip. Suniti wanted to hear some more. Who else could be better than Mr. Sharma? She positioned herself so that she could overhear Mr. Sharma once again. Mr. Sharma was standing with a stranger, probably an employee at the bank.

Suniti didn't have to wait much longer for the gossip to start. He asked Mr. Sharma, "Mahender has been very lucky. Do you know how Mahender got this job? I heard there was a big competition for the position!"

Mr. Sharma replied "It's an inside information. The foreign bank had three applications. All were great candidates. Vishal was the most suitable one."

"What? Then how did Mahender get it?"

"Honesty won, once again!" said Mr. Sharma with a very poetic tone. Suniti was listening very carefully with full attention.

"What do you mean?"

Mr. Sharma continued with a wink, "Confidential information. Don't tell anybody. The foreign bank wanted police checks for all candidates and references. Even though Vishal ji was more experienced and better qualified, he had a scarred police record. He was once accused of taking bribe from one of his clients and there is a police case filed. Mahender's records were clean. So, he got it."

Suniti was happy once again. Now she was seeing the rewards of being honest. She wasn't the richest woman in the party, but she definitely was the happiest one.

She realised that being honest wasn't bad after all. Honesty was paying them back. The rewards of honesty were very clear, a new job with a promotion and a good lifestyle in Australia. She appreciated it.

A week later Mahender caught his first overseas flight to Australia. He realised a few absurdities of Australian weather, culture and economics. It was summer in Australia, while it was winter in India. Nobody cared about what family background you come from, and it didn't matter whether you worked in an office or as a labourer, you visit the same pub for a drink. All had the same status, and he would be able to buy a lot more in India with his Australian dollar salary.

He rented a 3-bedroom house and slowly settled down. He bought most of the furniture, crockery, and white goods from local supermarkets. It was another four months before Suniti and the kids were going to join him. He didn't like eating out, so he started cooking. He realised he wasn't a very good cook. During those 4 months he lost more than 10 kilos.

It was in June that Suniti was flying in from India with the girls. The girls' annual examinations were over. Suniti didn't want to resign from her work, so she applied for long service leave. She sold their car and locked the house and handed over the keys to their close family friends to look after.

This was their first flight out of the country. They landed at the Tullamarine Airport, and it was freezing cold. Mahender was happy that the family was together again.

Hope for Others

Life went on. Mahender and Suniti were now settled in Australia. Mahender had completed his project successfully and started another project. They had bought a beautiful house with a big garden.

Suniti was still in touch with her NGO friend back in India. She did voluntary work for her as and when required. She loved working for the poor children.

Chanda went to college and Tara was still in school. They were now quite independent and didn't need their mother much. So, Suniti had a lot of time for herself. She thought of doing something more meaningful with her life.

Suniti loved the way Australians lived their lives and appreciated each other's cultures. They believed in mutual respect and equal opportunity for all. She knew she could get help from Australians for the children back in India if she made a genuine effort.

Suniti started an organisation called 'A Better life' through which she raised money for poor children in India. She helped many NGOs in India too. She connected the Australians with the poor and underprivileged children in India. She became the 'Hope' for every little child who didn't have a family and wanted to go to school.

In a short span of three years Suniti changed the life of thousands of poor children in India and other third world countries across the world. Her work was recognised and widely appreciated.

She meant hope for so many but one winter morning, she had to come to terms with the fact that she had little hope left for herself. This heart-breaking message was conveyed to her and Mahender by her doctor!

One day while on a walk in the park she felt dizzy and lost consciousness. One of fellow walkers brought her home. Mahender got worried and wanted to take her to the hospital, but she didn't want to go. She felt fine after some time. After a few days it happened again. This time Mahender didn't listen to her. He took her for a check-up.

After a few tests she was diagnosed with blood cancer. It was in its final stages. The doctor didn't lose hope though. She started her treatment schedule with regular chemotherapy sessions and medicines. "She doesn't have much time left," her doctor told Mahender.

Final Notice

Mahender was devastated. He could never think of a life without Suniti. He didn't know what to do! Suniti understood that she had to remain cool and take charge. Her family needed direction.

Mahender became much quieter. One morning Suniti noticed that Mahender was teary eyed. She laughed and said,

"Why are you crying?" she asked. Without waiting for him to respond, she continued, "I am lucky I have been given a notice. Tell me how many get to know their date of expiry? Most have to leave all of a sudden and then they can't rest in peace. I am thankful to God; he has given me some time. I must wrap up quickly and finish all the pending work. And I need your help in completing my duties."

Mahender and the girls were listening quietly. They were amazed to see the strength and the positivity Suniti had, even at a time when death was knocking at her door!

Suniti made a list of things she wanted to do. On top of the list was Chanda's wedding and it ended with Tara's. The other important work was appointing a board of trustees for 'A Better Life" her NGO. The other things in the list included visiting her favourite places, planting some fruit trees, and training Mahender how to cook.

Chanda, after finishing her graduation in journalism, was working for a media company. She was doing well and kept busy. Tara, on the other hand, was busy with her thesis for her master's degree. She would work and get busy after her course was completed.

Suniti was worried that Mahender would be left all by himself. She worked out a plan and talked to him one morning, "Listen, how about you start your own hockey club for kids. I know you always wanted one." Mahender had tears in his eyes. He knew the Hockey Club was for him to keep busy after she was gone! Mahender agreed.

She conveyed the message to the kids, "Why a Hockey Club mom?" asked Tara. "It is for your papa. He wanted to be a player, but he had so many responsibilities in life; he couldn't take the risk of being a player, he wanted Chanda to play

Hockey but she was never interested in games. We can have a club where your papa will teach little children to play hockey. I had planned this as his retirement gift, but I don't have that much of time!" Everyone listened to her in silence.

The news of Suniti's illness spread within their friend circles. They would occasionally visit them. By this time Mahender and Suniti had started talking to their friends about a suitable boy for Chanda. All the friends were talking about it. Chanda was intelligent and beautiful. Some of the friends also introduced suitable boys, but Chanda rejected all of them.

One night one of Mahender's old friends, Mr. Chawla called him and invited them for dinner. Mahender wasn't very keen, but he insisted. Though reluctant, Mahender agreed.

They all visited Mr. Chawla for the dinner. Chanda was introduced to Mr. Chawla's son Mahesh. He was a handsome young doctor. The evening was normal, however, everything changed when Mr. Chawla said "Mahender ji, *bhabiji* lets go to the other room and let them talk." He turned towards Chanda and continued "*Beta* (child) you two can talk freely." Chanda knew for sure that it wasn't a normal meeting. The elders were trying to fix their marriage. She was angry but decided to continue talking. Everyone looked very happy after the meeting except Chanda, she looked worried. She was quiet on her way back home.

The next morning Chanda came up to Mahender. She looked upset, "How could you do this to me daddy?"

"What did I do?

"You knew all the way! How did you think that I would agree to an arranged marriage? How can I marry somebody I don't even know!"

"Well to be honest, even I had no idea Chawla ji had this in his mind." Mahender said.

"Oh sorry, I thought you knew it and didn't tell me."

"But think about it. You don't have to marry straight away. You can meet him and get to know him. He is a doctor, very smart and well behaved."

Chanda rejected, "That's not possible" and went to work.

Suniti was observing quietly. She said, "You know she is an independent girl. I am sure she has her own choice. Maybe we should ask her if she has somebody in mind." Mahender nodded.

That night while having dinner, Mahender asked her if she had anybody in mind. Chanda was quiet. Suniti looked at her and said, "well…you know very well; I don't have much time left. I want to see you get married before I leave. So please don't keep quiet." Chanda wanted to talk but she was hesitating. Suniti could sense that, but she kept quiet too. After everybody went to their room, Suniti quietly walked into Chanda's room. Everything got very clear. She was right. Chanda loved a man from her work and wanted to marry him.

Without wasting any time, she broke the news to Mahender. The next morning while Chanda was having her breakfast, Mahender walked in, "Call Michael home on the weekend. We will talk. We will have an elaborate Indian dinner for him. I will ask Tara to make a nice dessert for this special occasion. She is very good at making desserts."

Chanda was surprised, "So you are not angry with me?"

"No," Mahender replied with a smile.

"What? Even though he is not Indian!"

"Yes, it's fine. But he has to prove to me that he loves you."

Chanda smiled, "Yes of course!"

She hugged Mahender with tears in her eyes. She whispered, "I love you so much. You are the best."

"Well, he has to be better than me and only then will I hand over my precious daughter to him," said Mahender.

Michael came home on Saturday evening. He was a handsome well-mannered young man with a soothing personality.

Suniti didn't want to waste any time, she asked, "Do you love my Chanda?"

"Yes, I do," came the prompt answer.

"When do you want to get married? I do not have much time and I want to see my princess married before I go!" Suniti asked.

"Whenever you say. I am ready," Michael answered. Everyone was quiet with eyes filled with tears and a smile on their lips. They all sat around the table as a family and enjoyed an elaborate dinner. After they finished, Mahender stood up, "Ok ladies, I will be taking Michael away from you. I want to have a man-to-man talk with him."

Michael followed him to the separate sitting area. The women were waiting for the outcome of the meeting. Chanda was kind of restless. The meeting seemed never ending. Chanda was getting very anxious. She couldn't wait any longer. She walked in. She was dumbstruck. She couldn't have imagined what she saw. Mahender had opened his most precious Champagne from his premium collection, and they were talking as if they were long lost friends.

Chanda was relieved, "I am sure Michael has convinced daddy" she smiled.

Chanda and Michael got married the next month. Mahender made sure that Suniti's family was there for the marriage. He wanted Suniti to meet all of them. Mahender's mother and sister also visited them. Everyone was sad. They were in no mind for a celebration. But they did everything as Suniti said. Suniti did every ritual for her daughter's marriage. Mahender couldn't take his eyes off Suniti. She still looked gorgeous.

Everyone went back after the wedding. Chanda shifted to Michael's house. Time was running out and a lot of Suniti's wishes had to be fulfilled. Mahender decided to take some time-off from work and spend time with Suniti.

Spending time with Mahender had been Suniti's foremost wish all her life. She was very happy. They planned to visit some of their favourite places not very far from home.

They went on a drive on the great ocean road, visited the Phillip Island to see the fairy penguins and the Yarra valley wineries. Suniti loved being with her family. Mahender held her hand throughout. He would never let her go if he had the option!

Mahender and Suniti had already started their work on two projects which were very close to their heart. Appointing a board of trustees for 'A better Life' and laying the foundation for the 'Hockey club for children.' Michael being the newest family member helped Mahender. He also agreed to be his assistant for the Hockey club. He used to play hockey in school.

After much thinking, Suniti decided to make Tara her successor of 'A Better Life'. Tara was undertaking research work in Psychology. She was sensitive and caring and took interest in her mother's work. She also made a trustee of five members including Mahender.

Suniti and Mahender met the local council and discussed their plan with them. They were interested and promised to support them actively. Suniti had a strategy ready. The plan was slowly taking shape. Chanda and Tara helped spread the word about the new hockey club and Michael helped make the website.

Children joined the club and Mahender was teaching them hockey, his favourite game! Suniti went with Mahender on many evenings. She sat there and watched Mahender interact with the children. She knew after she was gone, hockey was going to be his new partner in life.

Suniti's duties were all over except for Tara's marriage. She talked about it a few times, but she wasn't ready yet. They were all worried about Suniti. She was not keeping too well. The therapies and medicines had made her very weak and tired.

As time passed, she could not go to the hockey club anymore. She remained in her bed most of the times except for every morning when Mahender made her sit in the garden. She loved to watch her plants and the birds. They would hold hands and remember their old days. They laughed and cried as they recollected the special moments spent together.

Through many ups and downs, they had finally created their love story.

As Suniti's situation got worse, Mahender wanted to take a break from hockey. Suniti insisted that he should never take leave from hockey. One day Mahender wasn't feeling very good. Suniti thought he was making up a drama and wanted to spend time with her. She insisted, "The children will be waiting for you! They will be sad… Don't worry I will not go; I will wait for you to come back." That afternoon, Suniti passed away while Mahender was at the Hockey club.

She broke her promise, she didn't wait for him. Mahender now had to walk alone. He had learnt the skills from Suniti.

He did well. He got Tara married, kept his family together and fulfilled his duties at 'The Hockey Club' and 'A Better life.'

Yamini's 21ˢᵗ Celebrations Continue…

It was the next morning. All the young and old gathered around Nanaji to listen to his story. Nanaji described each of the four golden rules love, knowledge, hope and honesty giving examples from his life. Everyone loved Nanaji's stories.

They all agreed to Nanaji's golden rules of happiness and that 'The Golden Key' lies in our hands.

Mahender said, "I was lucky I got a life partner like your Naniji."

Yamini smiled and said, "Yes. When you get a good partner, you create lasting love and only then can you bring hope for others."

Everyone clapped at Yamini's words.

Nanaji joked, "She is not mini (little) anymore, she is maxi, and she has 'The Golden Key'. So, everyone be careful!"

Chanda walked into the room. 'The Spice Connect' people had arrived with lunch.

Mahender got up and went to receive them. Nandini was there with their order. She smiled at Nanaji and said, "This is the first time we are catering. I hope we meet your expectations!"

"You surely will my dear. I can see the love and commitment in your work."

Nandini with the help of her staff arranged their signature fusion dishes on the table. She explained each fusion dish in detail. Everyone was happy and hungry after seeing the spread.

As everyone gathered to eat lunch, Mahender looked around the room, taking pride in the family Suniti and he had built on love, knowledge, hope and honesty. Life had been good!!

He then turned to the gathered family members and said, "Lunch time now. Please help yourselves. Hope you all like the food and experience the joy of fusion."